PECOS VENGEANCE

Gunfighter Jess Millard seeks a more peaceful existence in mining than the one he experienced whilst farming. But he is forced to take responsibility of a baby cruelly orphaned by outlaws. He enlists the help of a beautiful teenage girl and her kid brother, but they too are haunted by a violent past. Soon Millard has to fight to defend his homestead, his new-found family and even the township itself against dangerous killers . . .

ROBERT EYNON

PECOS VENGEANCE

Complete and Unabridged

LINFORD
Leicester

First published in Great Britain in 1998 by
Robert Hale Limited
London

First Linford Edition
published 2001
by arrangement with
Robert Hale Limited
London

British Library CIP Data

Eynon, Robert
    Pecos vengeance.—Large print ed.—
Linford western library
    1. Western stories
    2. Large type books
    I. Title
    823.9'14 [F]

    ISBN 0–7089–4544–9

Published by
F. A. Thorpe (Publishing)
Anstey, Leicestershire

Set by Words & Graphics Ltd.
Anstey, Leicestershire
Printed and bound in Great Britain by
T. J. International Ltd., Padstow, Cornwall

This book is printed on acid-free paper

Dedicated to
Lyn Smith
for her help and encouragement

1

Formby stirred in his bunk and stretched his limbs contentedly. It was a nice feeling to know that you didn't need to start work for another four or five hours. He'd not even heard the early shift get up; the night air was chilly here in the mountains even this late in spring, so the old-timer had been snugly wrapped up in his blanket like a bug in an apple.

Outside, the rain was still coming down and it brought him his first concern of the morning. It hadn't let up all week and the miners had been complaining of the water level in the workings. Of course they'd grumbled about the possible risks, but in vain since Mr Weaver the mine owner rated each day by the amount of silver his workforce had produced. Above the sound of the rain Formby could make out the creak of the crushing wheel and the torrent of water and sludge in the washery chute.

Jess Millard was still asleep on the opposite bunk, his strong, angular face turned up towards the ceiling. Millard had been something of an enigma ever since he'd ridden up to the mine two months earlier in search of work. Although he had no experience of mining Mr Weaver had offered him a job. Millard was the sort of feller it was hard to refuse; now in his late twenties he was lean and tough even if he lacked the bulging muscles that constant physical work give a man.

Millard was honest too, and straight-talking though he kept apart from the usual disagreements and squabbles that divided the workers from the management of the mine. Indeed, Millard had knuckled down without a murmur and accepted the blisters and aching sinews till by now he was able to cope with most of the demands of his new profession.

As to the nature of his previous occupation the newcomer was quite uncommunicative, but it was not lost on anybody that he looked after his pearl-handled Colt .45 with as much care as if it had been his own child.

Formby was still wondering whether it would be better to roll his first smoke of the day or relapse once more into slumber when he heard an alarm bell being shaken frantically from the direction of the mine workings. In the far corner of the cabin someone cursed loudly and leapt from his bed. Formby threw his blanket to one side and sat up on the edge of the bunk.

'Wake up, Millard,' he shouted as he searched for his boots. 'That bell means trouble.'

A few moments later, wearing only his woollen underclothes and working-boots, the old-timer was out through the cabin door and trudging up the muddy slope leading to the entrance to the mine.

'Jesus . . . ' he muttered as he looked

up and saw water gushing from the tunnel and down the mountainside in a great, yellow flood. He knew at once what had happened: somewhere in the bowels of the earth a reservoir of rainwater had built up until the walls of the level had caved in under its pressure.

Standing at a safe distance from the torrent there was a group of helpless onlookers — smelters and washery-operators and miners who'd been fortunate enough to miss the fatal shift. They were staring and pointing at the course of the floodwater. Formby let his gaze follow theirs and suddenly felt sick in his stomach when he realized that the hillside was littered with the mangled bodies of men who had been his close friends.

Nothing could be done for the victims of the disaster who must have been drowned or crushed in a matter of moments, so Formby continued up the slope to where heated words were being exchanged between the workmen and

Mr Weaver's hired guards.

There were only two guards left at the mine; the others had accompanied Mr Weaver and a shipment of precious metal to Silver City a few days previously. Already the miners were concerned about their future and were demanding the payment they were owed, since the mine might never be workable again.

'We'll bury our dead,' one miner was saying, 'but after that want to be paid in full so's we can get the hell out of here before the whole mountain caves in on us!'

The two guards were unmoved. None of the miners facing them was armed.

'There'll be no decisions taken 'fore Mr Weaver gets back,' one of them informed the malcontents. 'And that's gonna take days.'

Both the guards were large men, and fleshy. Both wore guns and knew how to use them. Formby was listening so intently to the argument that he failed to notice Jess Millard had also climbed the slope and was standing at his shoulder. Millard had taken the trouble to dress and was even wearing his gunbelt.

'Well, I ain't waiting for no Mr Weaver,' the miners' spokesman said angrily. 'I reckon we're entitled to take what's owing us.'

He began to walk away; the rest of the workforce muttered their approval but none of them followed him.

'Where d'you think you're going?' the guard inquired sharply.

'To the office,' the miner replied without even turning round. 'Let's see what the pay-clerk has to say about it.'

One or two of the workmen began to stir. The guard realized he was close to losing control of the situation, so he drew his gun from its holster.

'You'd better hold it there, mister,' he warned, but the miner ignored the command and walked on.

Without compunction the guard fired once and returned his gun to the holster. The miner gasped and his legs buckled under him. He went sprawling into the mud and as he lay there a thin trickle of blood flowed from the corner of his mouth.

The guards turned again to face the crowd, who were visibly shaken by the suddenness of the killing.

'Do you understand now?' the second guard demanded. 'Nobody gets paid till Mr Weaver gets back.'

Then Jess Millard sidled past Formby and walked over to where the man lay.

'You volunteering to bury him?'

Millard turned towards the guards.

'Maybe,' he said in a deadpan tone. 'But first I'm gonna fetch my wages from the office.'

He moved away sideways, keeping the guards in his vision all the time. He could see the angry flush rise from their fleshy necks to their cheeks. That was good; they were losing their cool.

'You can fetch them all the way from hell,' one of the guards snarled. 'And I'm gonna send you there!'

Formby couldn't credit what happened next. He'd often seen Mr Weaver's men perform fancy tricks of gunplay to entertain and impress the miners, but now they looked gauche and stiff as they clawed for their weapons. Meanwhile, Millard had dropped on one knee and was already fanning the hammer of his .45. He only fired twice, since the guards hadn't had the sense to spread out. Each bullet hit its target with deadly accuracy; the two men landed flat on their backs in the mud, twitched for a few seconds and then became still.

Millard re-loaded the Colt and re-sheathed it without saying a word. It was Formby who broke the silence.

'We cain't hang around here; not after this,' he said. 'What d'you reckon, Jess, you got any suggestions . . . ?'

There was no resistance from the nervous little pay clerk when the miners presented themselves at the office and demanded their wages for the previous month. The petty official had heard the gunshots, and since no guards had shown up to control the workforce he deduced correctly that they were out of action and could no longer back him up.

He did raise an ineffective and feeble bleat when the men broke open the lock of the company store next to the office, but nobody paid any heed to him. The men were after dry clothing and liquor — and especially liquor, which was normally doled out to them sparingly, since heavy drinking was not conducive to hard work underground.

They also rounded up all the waggons, buckboards and pack-animals they could find. Only Jess Millard had a horse of his own, a gray gelding that accepted sun, rain or snow with equal stoicism. The departing band of miners opted to spend the first day's travel together. Despite their outward bravado they were an honest breed of men and they were secretly worried by the enormity of their crime. Although he'd played the principal role in the drama at the mine Jess Millard was inwardly the calmest of them; the way Millard saw it, he'd killed men before and not always in such a just cause as that morning.

That night they camped on a wooden slope. The rain had mercifully stopped falling but there was no way they could find dry fuel to light a fire. As compensation they cracked open some bottles of whiskey and rye and set about drinking to forget what had happened.

Millard didn't join them. Instead, he wrapped himself up in blanket and groundsheet and tried to get some sleep. However, the miners were talking too loudly and excitedly for him to drop off so he lay there watching the dark clouds scurrying across the broad canopy of stars above his head.

'Jess . . . ' The voice belonged to the old-timer, Formby.

'Yeah?'

'Mind if I settle down near you? It's a long time since I slept under the stars.

Don't want no coyote coming up and chewing off my arm in the night.'

'Settle down where you want,' Millard told him. 'There probably ain't much of the night left.'

He heard the old-timer wheezing as he laid out his bed. Years of mining had taken their toll of Formby's lungs. Even when he lay still Formby's chest was still heaving.

'That was mighty fine shooting this morning, Jess,' the old-timer said suddenly. 'You ever think of making a living out of your gun? Like lawmaking, for instance?'

During his time at the mine Millard had never discussed his past with anyone. Now it no longer seemed to matter.

'Sure, I've hired my gun out,' he admitted, 'but never as a lawman.'

'You mean you was a hired killer?' Formby asked bluntly.

Millard didn't reply, but the old-timer read his silence as a yes.

'What made you try mining, Jess?' he

11

asked. 'Must be easier ways for a feller like you to make a living.'

'Guess there may be,' Millard conceded. 'Only I cain't seem to find one; and gunfighting's strictly a young man's game.'

'Guess that's 'cause not many of them grow to be old,' Formby remarked and then chuckled at his own joke.

Millard was anxious to change the subject.

'Reckon the rest of them will be ready to move out at daybreak?' he said. 'No point in hanging about here to get caught.'

'Not much chance of that,' Formby replied sadly. 'They'll all wake up with sore heads tomorrow.'

Millard knew Formby was right. He also knew that his own safety was in jeopardy if he stuck too close to them. Next morning, when Formby awoke, Jess Millard was gone.

2

While Mr Weaver dined in style at one of Silver City's restaurants, in blissful ignorance of the events at the mine, outlaw Rafe Hollis and his gang were relaxing in much bawdier surroundings. The Flaming Horizon saloon stood on a corner of the main street and offered customers the rawest liquor and largest collection of soiled doves or prostitutes to be found in the booming township.

The saloon gave the same noisy welcome to all — alcoholics, sex-hungry cowboys and miners, outlaws on the run and those nondescript clients who sipped their cheap drinks timidly and were only there so that at some later date they could boast to friends and relations that they'd once frequented one of New Mexico's most notorious establishments.

Hollis was standing at the counter

and cradling a glass of whiskey in his hand; he was a small man, but by no means timid. Besides, he knew that he wasn't alone in the bustling room; four of his men, Taylor, Carling, Bebb and Franks were playing poker at a nearby table, pitting their wits against two of the professional gamblers the Flaming Horizon employed to fleece visitors of their payrolls.

The two remaining members of the gang, Diego and Randall, were not interested in cards. Diego was sitting near the swing-doors, enjoying a long-cheroot and watching the world go by. Randall, at twenty the youngest member of the gang, was in restless mood; he'd spotted a girl who'd taken his fancy as soon as he'd come into the saloon, but unfortunately for him she was already on her way upstairs with another client.

The girl and her client had been gone almost an hour and the young outlaw was getting more impatient every minute. Of course, there were other girls of the same sort in the saloon, plenty of them, but Randall had set his mind on that one girl in particular and he wasn't the sort of feller who'd be denied anything.

Randall was the only member of the gang who worried Hollis. The older man had formed the gang over a period of a year or so and had been readily accepted as its leader since he had the coolest head and was also the most experienced in bank robbery and stage hold-ups. His authority was only challenged when Randall got near a woman he fancied. Then his eyes would narrow and glow with a strange light and a nerve beneath his eye throbbed uncontrollably.

Hollis glanced across at the youngster, who couldn't keep still. The warning signs were there, already; if three U.S. marshals were suddenly to walk through the swing-doors, Randall would get to that girl before they took him in.

The card game was no problem. The

two gamblers specialized in cheating anyone who was drunk or foolish. They recognized their four opponents for what they were — hard, clear-headed men who'd gun you down without hesitation if you trifled with them. So tonight the gamblers forgot their sly tricks and played it straight. The saloon didn't pay them to get themselves killed.

At long last the man who'd gone upstairs with the girl came down again. He was unsteady on his feet and had obviously been drinking, which probably explained why he'd taken so long over the girl. He passed quite close to Randall but didn't even notice the malevolent stare the youngster gave him. Hollis tensed for a moment, expecting trouble, but the drunk carried on his way and straight out into the street without even looking back. The gang leader heaved a sigh of relief; it seemed crazy to him that Randall could get so het up over a whore. He feared that sooner or later the youngster's obsession would land them all in one whole lot of trouble.

The girl was the next to descend the staircase. Her thin cheeks were flushed, or maybe she'd rouged them again after her exertions. Her flimsy dress was creased and she was still smoothing it when Randall intercepted her. He spoke a few terse words to her, but they didn't seem to have the desired effect since the girl turned brusquely away and made for the counter where Hollis was standing.

Randall was too quick for her; in a flash he'd seized her arm and Hollis saw her face contort with pain under the pressure of his grip. Without ceremony the young outlaw almost dragged her backwards and forced her to climb the stairs at his side.

Nobody in the saloon seemed to notice or care about Randall and the girl, and Hollis relaxed again when they'd disappeared from his view. Hopefully Randall would satiate his lust on the girl and return in a calmer frame of mind. Hollis drained his whiskey-glass, then re-filled it from the bottle at his elbow.

Barely five minutes had elapsed when a terrified scream was heard that cut through the tinkling of the saloon piano. Doors slammed upstairs and there was a lot of shouting. Then two burly men appeared at the top of the staircase holding the writhing, fully-clothed figure of Randall between them. The pianist stopped playing and one of the men yelled down to the people below.

'The dirty scum . . . He was stripping and beating the girl for no reason!'

They negotiated the stairs with difficulty since the youngster was still struggling for all his worth. Then, halfway down the staircase, he became suddenly docile for a few moments. Confident that they were winning the battle the big man on his right relaxed and was hit off his balance when Randall threw his whole body-weight against him. The banister bent under the impact and then disintegrated with a loud crack. The man fell head first over the edge and smashed his skull on one of the oak tables below.

Randall started to pull away from the man on the inside. Both of them were armed and both went for their guns at the same time, but the contest was unequal: Randall's Colt levelled first and fired point-blank into the man's stomach. The man grunted and rolled forward down the stairs. Randall peered over at where his other assailant had fallen, but the feller was still out cold.

Hollis knew better than to give orders to the youngster when his blood was up. Instead, he nodded to Diego and the four card-players to indicate that it was time for them to leave. The stratagem worked; deserted by his partners Randall realized that he was alone and vulnerable in a hostile saloon. No town marshal was likely to trouble him for killing a man in a place like this; if any retribution was coming his way it would be here and now. He sidled his way over to the swing-doors, keeping his gun trained on the customers all the while. At last he was out in the safety of the night air where the others were waiting for him.

The next afternoon Hollis read with interest a notice in one of the town's store windows. A local mine owner, Weaver by name, was seeking to form a posse to hunt down a gang of renegade miners who'd raided his safe and ransacked the company store. Hollis decided that he and his men would be part of that posse whatever happened. Silver City was getting too hot for them, and especially for Randall. It was time for them to make for open country again, and this new venture offered them the chance to make some money while they were at it.

3

Weaver the mine-owner had given his hotel lounge as the assembly point for anyone interested in signing up for his posse. He was anxious to set out in pursuit of the renegade miners at the crack of dawn. His wages clerk had risked his life to negotiate the dangerous mountain paths that led to the nearest silver mine to Weaver's. He'd arrived there exhausted but able to blurt out the news of the flood and subsequent killings. A messenger had been despatched post-haste to alert Mr Weaver, but a couple of days had been lost already. The vengeful mine-owner needed men, and he needed them fast.

His own guards proved reluctant to commit themselves to the venture. Some of them had made enemies at the mine and they knew that the workers were fully armed. The guards agreed to return to the site of the disaster and clean up the mess; further than that they wouldn't budge.

By sunset only two volunteers had presented themselves at the hotel, and both of them were drunk and down-at-heel. Most folk were doing quite well for themselves in Silver City's booming economy; Weaver's terms were generous, but not generous enough to make them want to give up their comfortable lifestyle in exchange for hardship and peril.

Weaver curtly rejected the two drunks and was about to make his way to the hotel restaurant when Hollis and his gang strode in through the main door and announced that they were looking for the posse.

Weaver was not pleased to see the Mexican in their ranks. He was by nature prejudiced against all dark-skinned men, and he took Hollis to one side and told him of his reservations. Hollis looked shrewdly around the room for a sign of other volunteers.

Seeing none, he informed the mine-owner that either he took them all, or none at all. Weaver had no option but to agree and the terms were settled in a matter of minutes.

'You're a determined man, Hollis,' Weaver complimented him drily.

'We all are, Mr Weaver,' the outlaw replied. 'And I reckon that's the sort of men you'll be needing.'

Fortunately, the wages clerk had used his eyes and his ears when the miners had packed their bags and lit out. His message to his boss made it clear that the renegades were heading for flatter country to the south-east. When Weaver met up with Hollis and his men the next morning they were able to save valuable time by striking eastwards out of the township rather than return to the mine and begin the pursuit from scratch.

The mine-owner was disappointed to be riding alongside such a small band of men. He'd hoped for a posse of twenty at least, so that the fleeing miners would have been outnumbered almost two to one. He consoled himself with the thought that these riders seemed able and confident. They were certainly a rough, tough outfit and he was glad that Hollis exercised such obvious control over them.

The posse were fortunate to meet the occasional homesteader or traveller along the way who could confirm sightings of a dozen men or so riding a cavalcade eastwards. Then, on the third day they had a real breakthrough: as they approached a rivulet to water their mounts they stumbled across a lone rider who'd just opened a tin of baked beans for breakfast.

Before the poor feller realized what was happening he was surrounded by a gang of evil-looking strangers. Then Mr Weaver his former employer rode up and addressed him.

'Well, well, if it ain't Mr Formby.' Weaver said with a twisted smile. 'According to my wages clerk you lit out with the rest of them when the killing and looting was done.'

Formby's mind was racing as he rose stiffly to his feet. The old-timer knew he couldn't rely on denials to save his skin. He'd have to come up with something useful if he was going to win back the mine-owner's favour.

'I guess I didn't have much choice in the matter, Mr Weaver,' he said. 'They was all younger than me and their blood was up. They'd have killed me rather than leave me behind to bear witness against them. I got away from them the first chance I had.'

Hollis decided to take over the questioning. The miner's excuses would get them nowhere.

'D'you know where they're heading?' he asked.

'Sure I do.' Formby nodded his head vigorously. 'El Paso and the border. But you'll catch them before that. They been drinking since they left the mine and it's slowed them up.'

'Apart from you, Formby,' Weaver broke in sharply, 'have the rest of them stuck together?'

The old-timer didn't want to mention Jess Millard, because the gunslinger had stuck up for them all back at the mine. On the other hand he was scared to tell a lie, in case he was found out later.

'That new feller, Millard,' he said reluctantly. 'He only stayed with us one night, then he rode off on his own.'

'Well, I ain't splitting up the posse for one man,' Weaver said. 'We'll go after the rest of them.'

The mention of the name Millard stirred a memory in the Mexican's mind. A man called Millard had once helped him out in Wichita when a couple of Texans had taken exception to Diego's dark skin. Luckily for them, they'd backed down when Millard intervened. Luckily, because later that same day Diego had seen Millard gun down two men who'd drawn on him during a game of dice. Wyatt Earp was a deputy in Wichita at the time and he'd struck a deal with Millard whereby the latter kept his gun but left town next morning.

It couldn't be the same man, the Mexican reasoned. The Millard he'd known was a gunfighter, not a miner.

Meanwhile, Weaver and Hollis were holding a council of war, in which the outlaw showed himself to be the dominant partner.

'If they realize we're after them we're gonna lose men,' he told the mine-owner. 'I'll take four men along with me, and Formby can come as well. That way we'll know we ain't gunning down the wrong men.'

'What about me?' Weaver demanded.

'The rest of you can follow on slowly. And keep your eyes open in case your miners wander off course.'

Much to his annoyance, the young-ster Randall was left behind with Weaver and Taylor. Randall was still annoyed over his treatment at the Flaming Horizon in Silver City, and he wanted more blood. Hollis understood that and regarded it as a threat to his carefully-laid plan.

'You'll stay with Mr Weaver,' he informed the youngster curtly. 'If you don't like it, you can turn back.'

The young hothead bit his lip and said nothing. He knew the others would back Hollis up in a showdown. Well, that's OK, he thought bitterly to himself, but my day will come, Hollis, my day will come . . .

4

By riding hard for the rest of the day they caught up with their quarry by sunset. The posse spurred their mounts up a small elevation so that Formby could take a good look at the cavalcade from a safe distance.

'That's them,' the old-timer informed Hollis. 'They'll make camp soon; they don't like travelling in the dark.'

Formby was blissfully unaware that he'd just signed his own death warrant. He'd outlived his usefulness to the outlaws. Hollis nodded his head meaningfully and Bebb leaned across and threw his arms around the miner's shoulders. Before the old miner could make a sound the Mexican Diego had plunged his Bowie knife through his rib-cage and into his heart. Formby gave a little gasp and went limp in the saddle. Bebb released his hold and let the lifeless body fall to the brown earth below.

Ten minutes later the rear rider of the miners' cavalcade noticed a small group of men closing in on them from the western horizon. He shouted a word of warning to the others and several of them drew their guns in anticipation of trouble.

However, the greeting Hollis gave them was cheerful enough as he brought his horse alongside. The curious miners turned their attention to the swarthy Mexican who was riding uncomfortably with his hands tied behind his back. He was flanked by Carling and Franks while Bebb brought up the rear of the small party.

'We're taking a prisoner to El Paso,' Hollis announced by way of explanation. 'He's gonna be hanged for murder.'

The soberest of the miners was a man called Dibbens. Unlike his companions he controlled his drinking in the heat of the day, though he could drink with the best of them after sundown.

'What, you lawmen or something?' he inquired, wondering why none of them was wearing a badge.

'Bounty hunters,' Hollis replied smoothly, then added with a touch of humour. 'But don't worry, we only hunt redskins and greaseballs.'

Dibbens felt a sense of relief; the bounty hunter wouldn't joke like that if he'd had wind of the killings at the silver-mine. Besides, the stranger was very frank and talkative. He'd started to tell his life history already.

'I was in the cavalry for years,' Hollis confided. 'So were my friends here. We just kinda drifted into this when our army days were up. Guess soldiering don't equip you for a settled life in one place.'

The miner nodded in agreement.

'My brother was just like you when he came home from the Civil War,' he said. 'I found him a good job on a neighbour's farm, but he couldn't stick the boredom. One morning he rode off and that's the last we ever saw of him.'

Hollis glanced across at one of the miners who was raising a bottle to his lips.

'You should warn your friends to keep their wits about them,' he told Dibbens. 'The Navajos have been restless of late. They've burned some homesteads and attacked lone travellers. D'you post sentries at night?'

Dibbens shook his head. He was looking very thoughtful. They'd been so full of their other troubles they hadn't given Indians a thought.

'Well, I reckon it must be our cavalry training make us think like that,' Hollis remarked. 'It becomes second nature, and anyways I'd never take chances with a Navajo; They're a mean breed of Indian.'

He made as if to turn his horse away, but the miner reached out and restrained him for a moment.

'It ain't long off dark now,' Dibbens said. 'Why don't you make camp with us tonight? We got plenty of food and drink to share with you, and I cain't see any Indians risking attacking a big group of us.'

Hollis turned and consulted his fellow riders. To the miner's great relief none of them objected to the plan.

'We'll accept your offer of food,' Hollis said. 'We been living on hard tack for days. As for the liquor, we never drink when we're working. Besides, we'll be responsible for keeping watch tonight. That way you and your partners will be able to sleep easy without any redskin sneaking up on you . . . '

Despite the alcohol he'd consumed Dibbens slept fitfully in his blanket. All that talk about Navajos had troubled him and was giving him bad dreams. A strange sound jolted him out of his slumber and he rolled off his back onto his side. Then he heard it again — a sort of sigh or grunt; only this time it had shifted location a few yards.

He opened his eyes that were bleary

with liquor and sleep. The moon was full and was perched almost on the horizon so that it sent scary shadows along the silver-white earth. Someone was moving about nearby. He raised his head and saw a moustached face gleaming in the moonlight. His pulse raced as he recognized the man as the prisoner the bounty hunters were taking to El Paso to be hanged. The Mexican dropped to his knees beside him and Dibbens could see the blood dripping from the blade of his knife. The miner gave one last plaintive cry for help before Diego's knife sliced deep into his neck and silenced him for ever.

Carling, Bebb and Franks were prepared for the scream of terror when it came. Despite the Mexican's litheness of movement and skill with the blade, sooner or later someone was bound to give the alarm. The outlaws had positioned themselves to cover every corner of the encampment. As the miners threw their blankets to one side and fumbled for their weapons they were gunned down at nearly point-blank range by their tormentors.

It was all over in less than a minute. The smell of cordite and death reached the nostrils of Hollis who was sitting on a rock a little distance away, enjoying a rolled smoke. On one point at least he hadn't lied to his intended victims: Hollis had kept watch in case of an Indian raid.

5

After splitting from the miners' cavalcade Jess Millard made his way eastward through mountain range and upland plateau until he'd left the Rio Grande behind him and had entered the plains region watered by the Pecos river. He was in no great hurry because he'd long since lost any fear of pursuit, and he lacked neither provisions nor money.

Occasionally he'd call in at a small township and replenish his supplies; at other times he'd stop at isolated farmhouses where he'd usually be offered a bowl of stew and a hunk of home-made bread. The folk in these parts were generous to travellers; most of them had journeyed hundreds or even thousands of miles to reach the West years before, and the spirit of comradeship in adversity had never left them.

He arrived at one such homestead late one afternoon. The day had been torrid without a cloud in the sky. The welcome sight of a stone well greeted him as he rode past the corral where a couple of sturdy mares were drinking from a trough, while a small pig basked lazily in its shade.

Millard decided to ask permission before allowing his horse near the precious liquid. As he dismounted a short, stocky man aged about forty came out of the house to greet him.

'Afternoon,' Millard said. 'My horse could do with some water. Is that OK?'

The farmer looked him over carefully but without hostility.

'Sure it is,' he replied. 'The trough's full, and the water in the well is cool if you want to draw some for yourself.'

Millard thanked him and led the horse back to the corral. The animal drank greedily while his rider drew himself a draught of spring water with the help of a wooden pail he found by the side of the well. He could hear the sound of voices from inside the farmhouse. The homesteader was talking to a woman whom Millard couldn't see. Then the front door of the dwelling re-opened and the man walked over to the well.

'My wife will have a meal ready soon,' he informed the stranger. 'She says you're welcome to share it with us.'

Millard didn't need to think long about it. An hour indoors would revive his strength and spirits.

'That's mighty generous of you,' he said.

'You go on inside,' the farmer told him. 'I'll find some shade for your horse.'

The interior of the house was cool and shadowy after the bright sunshine of the afternoon. Millard stood in the doorway and let his eyes adjust for a few moments. A petite, attractive woman in her middle to late thirties was standing at a table kneading dough. Next to the table was a small wooden chair and in the chair there sat a young child who wore a simple pink gingham dress.

Millard was taken aback by the baby. He couldn't remember when he'd last been this close to one. He stared at it with a mixture of awe and uncertainty. The baby stared back at him and began to gurgle and point a chubby finger in his direction.

The woman saw the expression on the stranger's face and couldn't help smiling.

'It's the buckle on your gunbelt,' she explained. 'She's fascinated by anything that's shiny and bright.'

Millard reached into his pocket and fished out two new silver dollar pieces.

'How about these?' he said to the baby. 'D'you want them?'

The baby's eyes opened wide as the stranger dropped the money onto her lap. She picked up one of the coins and gazed at it with wonderment. Millard turned to face the child's mother.

'She's not going to try to eat it, is

she?' he inquired anxiously.

'No, she won't try to eat it,' the woman assured him. 'That's very generous of you, Mr . . . '

'Millard — Jess Millard,' he told her.

'I'm pleased to make your acquaintance, Mr . . . Jess,' she said. His kindness had won her over. 'I'm Amy Lennox and my husband's called Tom. This is Abigail, our daughter,' she added proudly. 'She's not twelve months yet, but she's still sharp as a tack.'

Her husband came in from the yard as she spoke.

'Ain't you asked the stranger to sit down yet, Amy?' he chided her, then he spotted the coin in his daughter's chubby hand. 'What you got there, Abigail?' he asked her, and she chortled away happily.

'It's a present from Mr Millard,' Amy informed him. 'And there's another one just like it in her lap.'

'I hope she gets lots more of them,' Jess Millard smiled. 'I reckon she's pretty enough to marry a millionaire.'

'So long as she makes a happy marriage,' Tom Lennox said, 'like her mother and me. That's much more important.'

He and Amy exchanged fond glances, and the newcomer felt a sudden pang of envy for their obvious closeness. His own life had many lonely and empty moments.

'Tom, why don't you take Jess outside and have a smoke and a chat before supper?'

Her husband nodded his head and led the stranger outside. They settled down in a couple of rickety chairs and Millard rolled smokes for them both as Tom Lennox watched the sun die sowly on the western hills.

'You got far to go?' the homesteader inquired after savouring his first pull on the cigarette.

'I guess I'm not heading anyplace in particular,' Millard confessed. 'Could be any township where I can find work.'

'If you keep on heading east for

another fifteen miles or so you'll get to Reposo,' Lennox said. 'That's Spanish for *rest*, and the town marshal, Reagan, follows it to the letter. Ain't no job of work too small for him to avoid it like the plague!'

He glanced sideways at his guest, whose eyes were heavy after a day's travel in the sun. The homesteader had thought of a way to thank Millard for his generosity towards the baby.

'You ain't gonna feel like riding after supper,' Lennox said. 'Why don't you stay the night here? I can only offer you the barn, but it ain't draughty and the straw is dry.'

Millard protested half-heartedly before letting himself be persuaded.

'I'll be up early,' he told the homesteader. 'I reckon I'll make for Reposo and see what's on offer there.'

'You'll have breakfast before you leave,' Amy Lennox said from the open window. 'Tom's taking us on a fishing trip in the hills and we never set out on an empty stomach.'

After breakfast the next day Tom Lennox hitched up the buckboard for himself, Amy and Abigail. Jess Millard rode with them as far as the trail, but then their routes diverged. They seemed genuinely sorry to see him go, and he would certainly miss their friendliness.

'May see you in Reposo,' Tom Lennox told him. 'We call in there once in a while.'

Millard had ridden about a mile when he heard the shots. There was a strong westerly breeze blowing and the sound could have carried some distance. He pulled up his horse and wondered if Tom Lennox had taken a pot-shot at some game. He remembered the homesteader loading a rifle onto the buckboard among the other things.

Another shot rang out and made him turn around. He knew that he couldn't just ride on. He had to go back and make sure that the Lennox family were OK.

6

Hollis had had the rare satisfaction for him of earning a sizeable amount of money legitimately, even if a dozen miners had died in the process. Having acquitted their obligation to Mr Weaver the gang took their leave of him and made once more for the open spaces.

Although Hollis was their acknowledged leader, each gang member expected to be consulted whenever a major decision was taken which affected their future. Therefore, Hollis held a parley to decide on their next destination and objective. Randall, the youngest and most volatile of the group, urged Hollis to turn west again and look for pickings in the rich mining townships of Arizona.

'Let's hit the banks,' he said eagerly. 'They gotta be bulging with dollars

44

the way things are.'

Hollis was more sceptical. In the boom towns the marshal or sheriff was fast becoming a political figure who could call upon an impressive force of deputy law enforcers whose expertise was gunplay. Pulling a robbery in a town like that was like sticking your head in a wasp's nest.

'Let's make for Mexico and hole up for a while,' Taylor suggested, and Carling nodded his agreement despite the black look Randall gave them.

'That's right,' Carling said. 'We got money; let's spend it.'

But Diego, who was himself Mexican, did not relish the idea. He didn't mind associating with his present company north of the border, but he didn't want to take them any closer to his home. Randall in particular could be trouble and Diego knew that his own loyalties would be called into question if there was a flare-up between the outlaws and his own people.

Hollis could read the doubt on the

Mexican's face and he could sympathize with Diego's emotions.

'We'd be a target south of the border,' the gang leader said, 'and especially if we was flashing greenbacks around. First night we'd get drunk we'd wake up surrounded by a company of Mexican troopers. We'd either have to fight or pay our way out of a trap like that.'

'What d'you reckon then?' Randall demanded aggressively. 'We gonna stay here forever?'

'I agree with Taylor; we oughta lie low for a while,' Hollis replied calmly. 'But let's go somewhere we know the language, so's we ain't likely to make a bad move.' He turned to Bebb and Franks. 'D'you boys remember a Kansan called Reagan who rode with us a couple of years back?'

'Sure I remember him,' Franks said. 'He was a big feller but he didn't have much guts.'

'That's him,' Hollis said with a smile. 'He liked the money but he couldn't take the life, especially when things got rough. Well, last I heard he'd got a job as a lawman in a town called Reposo near the Pecos.'

Bebb knew Hollis well enough to follow his train of thought.

'D'you reckon we should go look him up?' he asked. 'This Reposo sounds a nice place.'

'I reckon,' Hollis replied. 'I always did enjoy meeting up with old friends!'

★   ★   ★

It had to be Randall's mount that went lame after stepping in a gopher hole. Randall had to spend the rest of the day perched behind Carling and carrying his own saddle until his arm felt like dropping off. Hollis told him not to worry; they'd been travelling for weeks and Reposo was less than a day's ride away. Nevertheless, Randall got up in a black humour the following morning and could barely address a civil word to anyone.

A solution to the problem presented itself more quickly than any of them expected. It was Franks who spotted the buckboard trundling along in the glare of the morning sun, and pointed it out to his companions.

Hollis shielded his eyes with his hand. There were no riders escorting the buckboard.

'That's the answer to your prayers, Randall,' he commented wrily. 'All you got to do is take the horse from them.'

Tom Lennox was not unduly concerned when Amy drew his attention to the approaching riders. His homestead was on land owned by the rancher Matt Lamont and cowpokes often called on the Lennox family to break the monotony of patrolling the range.

He was less happy when the riders drew nearer. They were hard-faced strangers and he didn't like the way the youngest of them was staring at Amy. The riders drew up about twenty yards away and Hollis didn't beat about the bush.

'We need a horse, mister,' he informed Lennox. 'So do me the favour of unhitching yours so's I don't have to cause you no trouble.'

Tom Lennox turned and muttered something to his wife. It was then that Taylor spotted the carbine lying between the two homesteaders, and concluded that Lennox intended to use it. Taylor carried two guns in his belt and drew one of them as the homesteader's hand hovered over the carbine. Amy shouted a word of warning to her husband and Lennox fatefully touched the rifle.

Taylor fired once and the woman slumped backwards onto the buckboard. Wild with shock and rage, Lennox brandished the carbine but before he could take aim Taylor fired again and the homesteader slid sideways on to the dusty trail.

Suddenly, the baby that had been lying asleep behind its parents awoke and began to cry out for its momma. The sound cut through Diego like a knife as he realized the enormity of their crime.

But Randall had other things on his mind. He'd leapt from the back of Carling's horse and now stood facing Taylor who'd sheepishly returned his Colt to its holster. The veins in Randall's neck bulged out and his lips were flecked with foam as he spoke.

'You sonofabitch,' he yelled at Taylor. 'Why'd you have to kill the woman? She's no good to us dead!'

There was absolute silence apart from the baby's crying. Taylor sat in his saddle like a statue, waiting for Randall's next move. Carling glanced across at Hollis, but the gang leader had already decided not to intervene. Randall was too far gone.

Taylor could read the challenge in the youngster's eyes and was determined not to back down. Hell, this had only happened because Randall had ridden his horse to death. He'd never liked Randall and right now he hated him. Taylor drew his gun smoothly, but

Randall was even faster. The youngster's first slug smashed into Taylor's right shoulder and paralyzed his shooting arm.

Randall had no need to shoot again, except that he was a born killer. He saw Taylor's Colt fall to the ground, then fired again, aiming for the outlaw's belly. Taylor doubled up with a low moan and slid slowly from the saddle.

Hollis waited for the last convulsion to subside in Taylor's body before he spoke.

'Well, I guess that solves the problem of the horse,' he observed philosophically. 'Now let's get out of here before anyone sees us. I never did hold with killing women.'

Randall walked over to where Taylor lay, but not to pay the dead man any respects; he picked up the Colt .45 that lay beside the corpse and stuffed it in his belt. It might bring him a few dollars in the next town.

7

The next few hours were like a bad dream for Jess Millard. By the time he reached the abandoned buckboard the outlaws were high-tailing it northwards. Bebb had spotted someone approaching from the east and the gang had taken evasive action immediately.

The scene confronting Millard filled him with revulsion and incomprehension. What had the homesteaders done to deserve this, and who was the stranger lying dead on the trail? Millard checked to see if Tom or Amy Lennox had survived the shooting, but both of them were absolutely still. Tom's rifle hadn't been fired, nor had the stranger's gun. He unsheathed the Colt and saw that a small letter T had been carved in the centre of its wooden butt. He wondered if the man had died trying to defend the homesteaders or had been killed accidentally by his cronies.

The baby was stirring again and calling for attention. Grim-faced, Millard dragged Tom's body on to the waggon alongside that of his wife. He'd need to go back to the house and get a blanket to cover them up, and then he'd take them into Reposo for the marshal to deal with it. Abigail was crawling about now; she'd have to be secured for the journey. The sweat ran down his face, not the sweat of physical but of mental effort. He gazed down at the baby; he'd never had this sort of responsibility before, but he knew he had to see the child safe. He owed that at least to the couple who'd been so good to him.

He climbed onto the buckboard and whistled for his own gray gelding to follow the buckboard.

★ ★ ★

If he hadn't had so much on his mind Reposo would have struck him as a nice town. Its main street was wide and straight and the saloons and stores were in good condition and prosperous-looking.

He passed an eating-house with tables laid out at the front. A few cowboys were enjoying their midday meal, and a slim girl with long brown hair was clearing plates away from the empty tables. She looked up as the buckboard trundled by and noticed the baby lying securely in its little cot. Her gaze met Millard's for a moment and he was struck by her dark beauty, then he felt a sharp pain of guilt as he thought of the seriousness of his mission to town.

The door of the marshal's office swung open as the buckboard ground to a halt outside. The marshal, a big man, was on his way to lunch.

'Is it important?' he asked irritably as the driver descended from the buck-board and blocked his path. Then he noticed the baby.

'I reckon so,' Millard replied, pointing to the blanket. 'I got the child's parents lying there. They were gunned down a couple of hours ago.'

The lawman raised his eyebrows and went over to the buckboard. He raised the edge of the blanket and examined the corpses.

'I know them,' he said. 'I've seen them in town from time to time. Quiet folk; didn't seem the types to make enemies.' He let the blanket fall into place again. 'You'd better come inside,' he said. 'Let's hear your story.'

Marshal Reagan sat in silence as Millard related events as far as he knew them.

'And this other feller who got himself shot, you never seen him before?' Reagan inquired.

'Nope; and it wasn't Lennox who killed him. Lennox's rifle hasn't been fired.'

'What about the other feller — did

you check his gun?'

Millard nodded. 'It was fully loaded,' he said. 'But he did have an empty holster, so maybe he was carrying two guns. The one I found had a letter T carved on the handle. It's out there on the buckboard.'

The lawman scratched his chin. All this had happened outside his jurisdiction; he didn't really want to get involved.

'You got two choices as I see it,' he told Millard.

'What are they?'

'Either you pay to get the Lennoxes buried on our Boot Hill, or you take them back to the homestead and bury them there.'

'The homestead?'

The marshal eyed him up and down. If this man wasn't a rootless drifter then he was a hen's claw.

'That's right, the homestead,' he replied. 'You got any better place to go?'

His visitor thought about it. He'd

almost forgotten that there were live-stock back there that needed tending. Everything that Tom and Amy had worked hard for would go to ruin.

'What about the baby?' he asked suddenly. 'What's gonna happen to her?'

The lawman shrugged his shoulders. 'Ain't no orphanage here in Reposo. You can try the pastor's wife if you like, but she's a hard woman to deal with.'

Abigail squirmed in Millard's arms as if to tell him not to hand her over to a stranger. He thought of the girl serving in the chop-house; she had a kind face. Maybe she could help him or direct him to someone who'd look after Abigail.

Meanwhile, Marshal Reagan had been doing some thinking of his own. If the body lying out on the range was that of a wanted outlaw there might be some reward money in it for him.

'Don't you worry about the feller you left out there,' he assured Millard smoothly. 'I'll send the undertaker to bring him in. You see, I can bury vagrants at the town's expense, but your friends there kinda had a place of their own on the homestead. By the way, mister, you got a name, just for my records?'

Millard carried the baby to the open door. 'Sure I got a name, Marshal,' he replied and then slammed the door shut behind him.

8

Millard brought the buckboard to a stop outside the chop-house where he could keep an eye on it. The marshal was still the only citizen of Reposo who knew that two dead bodies lay concealed under the blanket behind the driver's seat. He carried the baby to a shady part of the open terrace. As soon as the girl noticed him she dropped what she was doing and came over to his table. She stood there staring at him without saying a word, and he felt uncomfortable as if he and Abigail had no right to be there.

'I need help,' he told her frankly. 'I may have to look after this baby for a while and I ain't got much idea how she should be looked after and fed.'

The girl turned on her heels and walked past the tables and into the kitchen. A few minutes later she

59

re-emerged, carrying a bowl of broth and a small wooden spoon. She sat down on the bench next to Millard and raised a spoonful of the potage to the baby's mouth. Abigail accepted the gift readily. A few drops of the broth fell onto Millard's forearm, and he smiled because now he felt more a part of the operation.

'That's fine, Miss,' he complimented her. 'But you'll have to tell me what's in that bowl there so that I can make some myself when I get her home.'

A cowboy on the next table laid his *Reposo Chronicle* to one side and confided to the stranger,

'You won't get a word out of her, Mister. She's dumb; cain't speak a word.'

Millard looked at the girl in surprise and a veil of sadness passed across her features that added to her quiet beauty. Just then the swing-doors of a saloon across the street swung open and a big, bald man appeared. He walked, or lurched rather, in the direction of the eating-house.

'Better watch out, Maggie,' the cowboy with the newspaper warned the girl. 'Ned's been drinking again. You don't want to get on the wrong side of him.'

The big man staggered past without seeming to notice anyone. The talkative cowboy grinned behind his back.

'Ned's a nice feller when he's sober,' he told Millard. 'But drink gives him a temper he always regrets later.'

Ned disappeared into the interior of the kitchen, but not for long.

'Goddam it,' he yelled from the doorway. 'You gone and left the pan of fat on the fire. You're gonna burn my place down!'

There was a bucket of water standing near the door. The big man picked it up and hurled it into the kitchen. There was a sizzling sound and a great cloud of steam emerged and enveloped the upper part of his body.

The girl put the bowl and spoon down and hurried towards the kitchen, but another cowboy shouted to her to keep clear of her employer.

'I ain't smelled no burning fat, Maggie,' he told her. 'Ned's just drunk and trying to find fault.'

The big man turned on the cowboy with surprising speed, dragged him clean out of his seat and hurled him yards into the street. Then he advanced on the trembling girl.

Millard was on his feet, too. He dumped Abigail on the talkative cowboy's lap and strode deliberately into the path of the big man. Ned, however, was only interested in getting at the girl and he tried to hustle the stranger to one side, only to be rewarded by a short, straight jab in the ribs that made him grunt angrily. Then Millard hit him on the side of the skull, but the punch had no more effect than an insect sting.

Screaming with rage Ned lashed out wildly and struck Millard a hefty blow on the chest that sent him careering backwards against one of the heavy tables. Before the big man could reach him Millard had the presence of mind to grab hold of a chair and hold it in readiness. Assuming that his opponent meant to swing the chair at his head, Ned covered his face with his arms and rushed forward.

Millard saw that the big man was charging blindly, so he merely lobbed the chair at the feller's feet and slipped deftly to one side. When Ned's feet collided with the obstacle his balance went completely and he fell forward helplessly. Then Ned made the mistake of lowering his arms to break his fall on the floor. As he went down his unprotected head caught the edge of the table with a sickening thud. The scrap was over; Ned was out cold.

The girl, meanwhile, was scurrying along the sidewalk away from the chop-house. Millard retrieved Abigail with a word of thanks to the cowboy and went after Maggie. The pursuit took him almost the length of the main street and into a series of dingy backstreets and alleyways. Finally he saw her enter a building that was little more than a shack. The door wouldn't even shut properly so he followed her inside without waiting to be invited.

Maggie was sitting in a moth-eaten armchair weeping softly. At her side stood a boy of about six or seven years of age. He looked puzzled and anxious, but he was still grown-up enough to put his hand on the girl's shoulder in an attempt to console her. As she sat there, so slight and vulnerable, Millard found it hard to believe that she was the mother of a child.

The boy heard him come in and stared at him challengingly. He obviously thought that the stranger was harassing his mother.

'What d'you want?' the boy demanded, trying to make himself taller than he really was. 'Go away. Leave us alone!'

Millard scratched his head with his free hand. Luckily, Abigail was sleeping after her meal. He looked around him. The shack was clean but the furniture was old and rickety; he wondered if the roof kept out the rain.

'I'm sorry if I've lost you your job,' he told the girl. 'D'you reckon you can go back there?'

She dried her tears on a piece of cloth, then nodded her head. He wondered if she was just trying to make him feel less guilty.

'D'you want to go back there?' he asked.

She lowered her head. She seemed utterly resigned to whatever life threw her way.

'I can give you some money to get you by until you find another job,' he offered and she looked at him with surprise. 'Or else,' he went on awkwardly, 'or else you and your boy can come with me. I'm going to take Abigail here back to the homestead where she was born. Her folk have been killed and I've got to bury them. I'll stay there till things are sorted out, maybe longer. I got nowhere else special to go.'

He watched her closely and realized

suddenly that he was praying that she'd agree.

'Well, what's it to be?' he asked her after a few moments had elapsed. 'Do you want to take the money?'

She shook her head and that gave him hope. She looked up at the boy but he was impassive.

'I'm scared for the baby,' Millard said. 'I don't want anything to happen to her. Will you come back with us?'

This time the girl nodded her head, and Millard heaved a deep sigh of relief.

9

Fortunately, the girl turned out to be a competent rider and she rode Millard's gray gelding back to the homestead. She carried the boy behind her; in that way neither of them had to go too close to the dead bodies of the Lennoxes. For the most part they journeyed in silence, though Millard did manage to learn from the youngster that his name was Luke. The boy was uncertain how old he was but he could remember a time when his ma, or Maggie as he frequently referred to her, was able to speak. When Millard inquired as to what had happened to strike the girl dumb Luke averted his eyes and made no reply.

When they eventually reached the homestead Millard ushered them into the house and told them to make themselves at home. He was pleased to see that Maggie's first concern was for the baby. He left the three of them to settle in, and went to the barn to look for tools with which to bury Tom and Amy Lennox. The most suitable spot for the graves was a hillock a couple of hundred yards from the farmhouse. He drove the buckboard over there and dug for several hours until darkness had fallen. He laid the couple side by side and covered them with brown earth. His heart was heavy as he laboured, not only for his lost friends but also for their surviving daughter whose future was uncertain.

When he got back to the house he found that Maggie was boiling water for him to wash down. She also had a pitcher of cold water ready and he drank greedily. Despite her thoughtfulness she eyed his every movement warily and so did Luke, as if Millard was an intruder in their midst.

In fact, the girl looked so fearful that Jess Millard thought it was time to make the situation perfectly clear to her.

'I guess you've been in the other room,' he said to her. 'The bedroom I mean.'

Maggie nodded her head and waited for him to go on.

'Well, that's where you and the boy will sleep,' Millard told her, 'and Abigail, of course, if that's OK.'

She nodded again and he could read the relief in her face. He thought how beautiful and vulnerable she looked, yet when he looked at the fire she'd lit in the grate and smelled the pot of stew she was simmering he realized that she was also a practical person and used to hard work.

'I spent last night in the barn,' he went on with a shy smile. 'It ain't at all draughty and I slept just dandy. So that's where I'll be bedding down from now on. But if anything happens that scares one of you in the night, or if Abigail gets sick you get Luke to holler real loud and wake me up.'

There were some minor misunderstandings over the next few days, but with Luke's help Millard usually managed to work out what Maggie wished to explain to him. The girl was a competent housekeeper and the Lennoxes had kept the homestead well stocked with supplies, so Millard didn't need to take the buckboard to Reposo for several weeks. While Maggie tended the house and the two children Millard kept the livestock fed and began to plant the spring seeds that Tom Lennox kept stored in sacks in the barn.

Abigail was not neglected either; when Maggie was busy with other chores Luke took charge of the infant, watching that she didn't crawl into places of danger such as the fireplace or the yard when the animals were roaming free.

Occasionally Luke lent Millard a hand feeding the livestock or watering a newly planted seed-bed, but more often the boy stayed close to Maggie and Abigail in the vicinity of the house.

Millard welcomed Luke's help and made sure to thank him, even when the boy's efforts were clumsy and counter-productive; however, he could sense an unwillingness on Luke's part to draw close to him. It was the same with Maggie; he couldn't fault her as a housekeeper, but there was always a barrier between them and it got no easier as the days went by because his own feelings for her intensified to the point that he carried her portrait in his head whenever she was out of sight.

Almost a week went by before they received their first visitors, and then a half-dozen of them rolled up in a bunch. When the men rode up Maggie was sitting in a rocking-chair at the door of the house, sewing linen while Luke kept the baby amused by drawing pictures in the earth with a stick. Jess Millard had been chopping wood at the back of the house and he was still carrying his axe when he came round to the porch to greet the riders.

The front rider was a gaunt, gray-faced man in his fifties; his forehead was lined prematurely and he sat unnaturally stiffly in his saddle. He introduced himself as Matt Lamont and went on to say that he owned the surrounding land, including the plot where the homestead was located.

'My name's Millard, and the girl's called Maggie,' Millard informed the rancher. 'She's been helping me run the place since . . . '

'That's why I'm here,' Lamont interrupted him. 'I got word that Tom and Amy were dead, so I decided to come along myself to find out what happened.'

Millard invited the rancher and his retinue to dismount, but Lamont declined, saying that he was carrying an old wound from the Apache wars. He rarely got on a horse nowadays because any movement was painful. It was only his friendship for the Lennoxes that had brought him to the homestead on this occasion.

Millard related the story just as he'd told it to Marshal Reagan in Reposo, and more recently to Maggie and Luke. His telling of the bizarre and tragic event was so straightforward and bereft of elaboration that the rancher immediately accepted it as a true account of what had happened as far as Millard knew it.

'I'd like to see their graves,' Lamont said when the tale was told.

Millard nodded his head. 'They're over there on the hill,' he told the rancher. 'I ain't got round to putting crosses up. I thought I'd hang on till I can buy some hardwood in town.'

Lamont looked at him for a moment; the rancher was deep in thought.

'I hope you're gonna stay put for a while,' he said. 'You've gone some way to repaying the kindness Tom and Amy showed you. It'd be a shame if the place went untended.'

Millard glanced at Maggie, but the girl remained impassive.

'I don't know how much rent the

Lennoxes paid you, Mr Lamont,' he said, 'but I guess you'll be expecting the same from me.'

Lamont turned to the weatherbeaten veteran on his right.

'Tell him, Lew,' he said. 'You're my foreman.'

'Mr Lamont don't want no payment,' Lew explained. 'Only you'll notice that there ain't no fencing here apart from the corrals. That's Mr Lamont's rule: no fences on the open range.'

'I understand,' Millard assured him. 'I appreciate your generosity. I won't change things around here without asking you first.'

Meanwhile, a younger horseman on Matt Lamont's left was raising his hand and pointing to the baby playing on the ground.

'Don't forget what Ma told you, Pop,' he said. 'She reckons we should take the kid back to the ranch where it can be looked after.'

Lamont frowned; he was obviously less sure of himself concerning the care of young children than the fencing off of prairie.

'That's right,' he told Millard awkwardly. 'We reckon we owe it to Tom and Amy to care for Abigail there, seeing that they were such good neighbours.'

Maggie rose brusquely from her chair and scooped the baby up into her arms. She stood there defiantly, her eyes blazing with a mixture of fear and anger.

'Steady, Maggie,' Millard said in an even voice. 'I'll explain to Mr Lamont that you're real good to Abigail. He don't need to have no worries on that score.'

The rancher stared at the girl expectantly, waiting for her to speak out.

'She can't talk, Matt,' Lew explained. 'She's that dumb girl we've told you about, the one who was working for Big Ned in town.'

Lamont didn't look very convinced. 'But she's just a slip of a thing,' he objected, but then little Luke took a step forward.

'Well, she looks after me,' he piped up. 'And I ain't doing so bad!'

A smile lit up the rancher's face for a moment and wiped the lines of pain from his brow.

'I guess you win, Millard,' he conceded. 'You'll find my ranch-house five miles south of here. If you got any problems — and especially if Abigail falls sick — you get in touch with me at once. Understand?'

Millard fingered the rim of his Stetson to acknowledge his gratitude to the rancher.

'I understand, Mr Lamont,' he said. 'If Abigail gets sick, you and the doc will be the first to know about it.'

When the visitors had ridden off Jess Millard went back to his wood chopping at the back of the house. He'd split a couple of logs before he realized that Luke was standing nearby, watching him. Millard straightened his back and turned to the youngster.

'You did fine just now, Luke,' he complimented him. 'You stuck up for your ma real good.'

The boy lowered his gaze. 'I was real scared,' he admitted. 'There was too many of them for us to handle.'

Millard nodded his head gravely, then let his hand fall on the butt of his Colt.

'That's why men carry guns,' he told the youngster. 'A gun can make one man the equal of three or four in a fight. But first you got to know how to use it.'

Luke was staring at the holstered .45. 'Can I see it?' he begged. 'Can I handle it?'

'Sure.' Millard unsheathed the weapon and carefully emptied the chamber before handing it over to the boy. 'Don't go dropping it on your foot. It's heavier than it looks.'

Before they could complete the exchange, Maggie appeared from nowhere and thrust herself between them. Millard felt her slim fingers grapple with his and the effect on him was electric. It was the first time she'd ever touched him and his pulse rose sharply. In a flash she'd wrestled the Colt from his unresisting hand and thrown it violently to the ground.

He stared at her and was surprised by the expression on her face. It was as if she'd just touched the Devil, and he wasn't sure if the Devil was the .45 or himself.

'You shouldn't have done that,' he rebuked her gently. 'Luckily it ain't loaded. If it was it could have gone off and killed one of us.'

The girl seemed beside herself with anger. She seized hold of Luke's arm and tried to drag him away but the boy resisted vigorously.

'It wasn't Jess's fault,' he yelled at her. 'I asked him to show me the gun.'

He broke free and began to run headlong towards the copse of woodland which served as the main source of fuel for the homestead. Maggie just stood there, looking bewildered, lost and hurt.

'You stay here,' Millard told her. 'I'll go after him. Everything's gonna be OK.'

Luke had sought refuge under the spreading boughs of an old oak tree. He was sobbing bitterly; Millard sighed to himself and wished that he had more experience of young children.

'You shouldn't blame your mother, Luke,' he told the boy. 'She was frightened for you, that's all.'

Luke turned his head to one side to hide his tears.

'She . . . she ain't my ma,' he said between sobs. 'She ain't never been my ma. We been lying to you all along. I mean, I been lying to you. I was scared you'd leave me behind if you knew.'

Millard was perplexed. He went over and put a fatherly hand on the boy's shoulder.

'Go on, tell me, Luke,' he said. 'Don't be afraid. Whatever you say I won't leave you behind — ever.'

The youngster took a moment to wipe his face on his shirtsleeve.

'Maggie's my sister,' he said at last. 'She looked after me after Pa got killed. She looked after both of us.'

'Do you remember your pa getting killed?' Millard asked.

Luke shook his head a little too vehemently. Millard guessed he was lying but he didn't want to push the kid too far.

'Well, now Maggie's looking after both of us,' Millard said cheerfully. 'Let's pull together and make things easier for her.'

'She likes you, Jess,' Luke said suddenly. 'I know she likes you, only she cain't tell you.'

Millard felt the blood rise to his cheeks. He needed to change the subject.

'Next time I go to town, you're coming with me, Luke,' he said.

'Me . . . what for?'

'You can choose a Bowie knife for yourself in the store. I'm gonna teach you how to carve and fashion wood so's you can help me make furniture for the house. Would you like that?'

'Sure.' The boy was smiling now. 'I'd like that, Jess!'

10

Marshal Reagan was half asleep in his leather-backed chair in Reposo's jailhouse, when the street door burst open unceremoniously and made him blink irritably in the sunlight.

A blond, lean youngster strolled into the room, smiling sardonically as if it was a big joke to wake the lawman up like that. Reagan was sore enough to reach for the .44 that he kept handy in a drawer at the side of the desk. Then the hairs rose at the back of his neck as the intruder drew his Colt with the speed of a striking rattle-snake.

As the town marshal stared into the barrel of the Colt two more strangers came into the office; one of them was tallish and fair-skinned, the other short and swarthy with distinct Mexican features. Then Hollis made his entrance, flanked by the remaining members of the gang. Reagan looked at him in disbelief.

'Yip, it's me,' Hollis assured him. 'I guess you remember Franks and Bebb.'

The gang leader motioned to Randall to put his gun away, and Reagan breathed more easily. He'd never fallen out with Hollis, and anyway his old compadre had a friendly smile on his face as he pulled up a chair and sat down opposite the lawman.

'We're planning to rest up for a while here in Reposo,' Hollis informed him. 'So I thought I'd look you up and find out what's what in the town.'

Reagan glanced around the room; Hollis always had known how to pick reliable and useful gunslingers and this particular bunch looked well up to standard, though the young blond feller seemed rather too gun-happy for comfort. He only hoped that they weren't in Reposo to cause trouble.

'Sure thing, Hollis,' he replied with a

forced smile. 'Anything you want to know — for old times' sake.'

Hollis raised his eyebrows; the last time they'd been together Reagan had high-tailed it into the hills because he thought a county sheriff was planning to arrest them. However, this was no time to pick at old sores.

'Well, for a start we're looking for somewhere reasonable to stay; and, of course, the horses will need to be looked after. D'you know anyone who's likely to give a good deal on account of us being such good friends of yours, Reagan?'

Reagan thought for a moment. Pearce at the Red Sunset saloon owed him a favour or two, and then there was Giles, who ran a stable less than a hundred yards from the Sunset. Giles was a drunk, and very open to persuasion if a whiskey bottle was waved under his nose.

'I'll see what I can do,' the lawman promised. 'I think you'd better let me do the arranging.'

'That's just dandy,' Hollis assured him, then glanced meaningfully in Randall's direction. 'Of course, we don't want to run up against any trouble during our stay. So if you know of anybody who's likely to take exception to us being here, you'd better give us fair warning so that we can keep out of their way.'

Reagan was pleased to hear the last remark. He was the ideal kind of lawman for a sleepy township like Reposo. He hated to think what would happen if things hotted up and got out of control.

'There's a group of young fellers who run wild from time to time,' he told Hollis, 'but they don't do no real harm, only stir things up a bit. The leader's called Jamie Lamont, only son of Lamont the rancher. Jamie's mother dotes on him and his father don't always feel well enough to keep the kid in line. Him and his friends have a liking for strong liquor, though they ain't out of their teens yet. When they've had a bellyfull they start getting up to their horseplay. Good thing is they always hand over their guns in the first saloon they go into. That's my rule as far as they are concerned. If you do run into them a good clip will put them in their place; there ain't no call for gunplay. Besides,' he added, 'Mr Lamont wouldn't approve, and he's got lots of influential friends in the territory.'

'So Lamont owns Reposo,' Hollis observed with a trace of sarcasm.

'Nope, he don't,' Reagan replied. 'He's got the oldest ranch in these parts, but the Double Q is the biggest. That's owned by Mr Quelch, a Yankee. Recently Quelch has taken to fencing off some of the approaches to the river. Lamont don't like that much.'

'What's he doing about it?'

'When he sees them he tears them down. Rumour has it that Quelch is looking for guns to back up his fence erectors.'

Hollis was looking very pensive; he

was thinking that if things didn't work out for them in Reposo they might be able to find a little excitement on the range — and even get paid for it.

11

Jess Millard was as good as his word; when the last sack of flour was used up he took Maggie and the two children into Reposo on the buckboard to stock up on supplies and also to buy Luke the Bowie knife he'd promised him.

In order to avoid another scene like the one over the Colt .45 he'd carefully explained to the girl the usefulness of a good knife in the countryside and this time Maggie had registered no protest. Her fear seemed confined to guns and Millard wondered what had instilled that fear, since guns were commonplace items in the frontier West.

When they reached town they toured the stores in search of goods and foodstuff that would tide them over the weeks ahead. Maggie played an active part in the proceedings, indicating by gestures of the hand and facial expressions what she considered a good buy and what she thought unnecessary or overpriced. When the buckboard was fully loaded it began to rain lightly and the dark clouds on the hills to the west indicated that there was worse to come.

'Why don't you take Abigail into the coffee-shop?' Millard suggested. 'Luke and I are going to the hardware store to pick him up a knife. It won't take long.'

He handed her some money and she smiled her appreciation. That was one of the things he liked about her: she was always grateful for every little thing he did for her, as if she hadn't always been used to kindness from men in the past.

The storekeeper, a bluff, bald old man, knew Luke by name, and he inquired straightaway about the boy's sister Maggie.

'I never thought I'd miss her,' he remarked, 'not with her being so quiet, but Big Ned's place just ain't the same without her. Ned's sorry now about losing his temper with her. I reckon he'd take her back in a shot.'

Millard made no comment; Big Ned's loss had been his gain. He asked the storekeeper to show them some knives and young Luke's eyes popped as an impressive display was laid out on the counter for his perusal.

'Now don't you get touching them blades,' the storekeeper warned the boy. 'Some of them knives would slice through your hands like butter!'

Millard left them to it and went over to look at a glass case that was full of handguns. It was only recently that he'd become a farmer and his gunslinger past still haunted him. He was still fascinated by the array of Colts behind the glass. Suddenly he noticed that one of the .45's had a distinctive letter T carved on its wooden handle. It was the twin of the gun he kept in a drawer back at the homestead — the gun he'd found on the unidentified corpse the day the Lennoxes had been murdered.

'This Colt?' he asked, pointing at it with his finger. 'Where'd you get it?'

The storekeeper sauntered over. 'The

one with the letter carved on it? A blond-haired feller sold it me a couple of days ago. He's a stranger in town.'

'Is he still around?' Millard asked.

'I reckon so. I saw him this morning with some other fellers I ain't seen before. They were talking to the marshal and they seemed right friendly with him, though they wasn't the types I'd choose for friends, if you know what I mean.'

When Luke had chosen the Bowie knife he wanted, and received a generous discount from the store-keeper, Millard took him back to the coffee shop and put him in Maggie's safekeeping.

'I won't be long,' he told the girl. 'I just got to talk to the marshal before we ride out.'

Reagan was puffing away contentedly at a cheroot and reading the local gazette when Millard walked into the jailhouse. The lawman never forgot a face and he gave his usual bland smile of welcome.

'Howdee,' he greeted his visitor. 'How's things on the homestead?'

'Just dandy,' Millard assured him. 'Maggie and Luke have settled in fine and the baby's growing every day.'

Reagan looked at him quizzically; Millard didn't look like a social caller.

'Anything on your mind?' he asked.

'Yip, there is one thing,' Millard replied, taking a seat opposite the marshal. 'D'you remember the gun I told you about, the one with the letter T carved on it? Well, its twin sister is over in the hardware store. It was handed in by a young blond feller that you were seen talking to this morning — him and a couple of his friends. They're strangers in town.'

Reagan's smile had turned into an irritated frown. The lawman hated complications. He felt like telling his visitor to mind his own business, but Millard didn't look the sort who'd be easily intimidated.

'That man you found dead,' he said slowly. 'After we brought him back to

Reposo for burial, I went through every wanted notice in my office to check him out. He fits the description of an outlaw called Taylor who carries a five hundred dollar reward on his head. I've filed for that reward with the County Sheriff. When the money comes through at least a hundred of them greenbacks will be yours.'

'What about the youngster who sold the gun?' Millard asked obstinately.

'Well, if he did kill Taylor I reckon he did us all a big favour,' Reagan replied philosophically. 'Besides, he ain't the sort of feller I'd want to pick a fight with, not unless I had good cause.'

Millard stared at him. 'So you ain't even going to question him or his pardners?' he asked.

'Darned right I ain't; and I advise you keep away from them if you got any feelings for Maggie and them two strays of yours.'

Millard thought over the lawman's words as he walked through the rain towards the coffee-shop. For the first time in years he felt the weight of responsibility on his shoulders. On the one hand he wanted to bring the killers of Tom and Amy Lennox to justice; on the other, how would Maggie and the kids fend for themselves if he got himself shot?

The sound of shouting shook him out of his reverie. Young Luke was in front of the coffee-shop doorway, yelling and tugging at three drunken youths who'd linked hands to form a circle around a tearful Maggie, trapped between them and protectively clutching the baby in her arms.

'Come on, Maggie,' one of them challenged her. 'You only got to open your mouth and ask us to let you go. You lost your tongue or something?'

Millard quickened his stride. On reaching the group he tried to wrestle his way inside the circle but the rain was falling steadily and it was hard for him to get a grip. Maggie turned her head towards him and he could read the panic on her face. Without regard to the consequences he swung hard at the side of the nearest youth's head. The lad staggered sideways and released his hold. Millard saw a clenched fist heading his way and he stepped in quickly and gave his attacker a short, vicious jab in the solar plexus. The youngster fell to his knees, coughed several times and began vomiting onto the damp earth.

It was only then that Millard recognized him as Jamie Lamont, the son of Lamont the rancher who also owned the land housing the Lennox smallholding.

On the far side of the street, obscured by a pillar of the Red Sunset saloon, the blond outlaw Randall was watching the scene with interest. He'd never expected to meet the girl again and he was anxious for her not to see him — not yet at least. But already the old lust was burning in his body and he knew that soon it would take him over completely even if he had to kill to satisfy it.

Diego the Mexican was also watching events through the window of the saloon. He recognized Millard as the gunslinger who'd sided with him in Wichita. Diego was ready to return the favour now, but Millard was well in control and needed no help. Well, maybe another day, the Mexican told himself . . .

12

The ride home in the driving rain proved too much for Maggie's constitution. In her eagerness to keep house well and to be a good foster-mother to Abigail the girl had neglected her own need for relaxation and sleep. For his part Millard had had to adapt to a new kind of life on the homestead and work out the best way to organize the tending of livestock and the growing of crops. That didn't leave him much time to concern himself with how Maggie was coping; meals were always on time and the baby was thriving, and that was good enough for him.

He first noticed that the girl was shivering as she added paper and dry wood to the embers of the fire she'd lit earlier in the day.

'Are you OK, Maggie?' he inquired, and then hurried out again to take the horses into the stable and rub them down.

Although she managed to prepare food for them all, Maggie felt too ill to eat any of it. Instead she went to bed and soon developed a raging fever. Luke took fright at her tossing and turning and he kept asking Millard if his sister was going to be all right.

'Sure she is, Luke,' Millard told him, wishing that he could convince himself as well.

He piled clothes on her when she complained of the cold and gave her water when her temperature rose. Although he was dog-tired himself he didn't leave her side.

'Keep the fire going, Luke,' he told the lad. 'That'll keep the air dry.'

In fact, all he wanted to do was to keep the lad busy so that he'd stop fretting. Eventually exhaustion overtook the boy and he fell asleep in front of the fire he was stoking.

It was almost dawn before Maggie also fell into a slumber that was deep and untroubled. Millard took advantage of the lull to go into the other room and make himself a bowl of coffee. His eyes were red and his head was aching but it wasn't worth him thinking of getting some sleep for himself. Soon the farm would be coming to life and there would be another day's work to get through. He shook Luke's shoulder gently and the boy opened his eyes.

'I got things to do, Luke,' Millard told him. 'You'll have to watch over Abigail and your sister and let me know if anything's wrong.'

Luke nodded his head. Despite his tender years he was already used to helping Maggie, and that included preparing food for the baby.

'You go ahead, Jess,' he assured Millard. 'I'll see to things here.'

Millard felt a warmth in his chest; Luke was doing his best to appear like a grown man, though he was obviously scared for his sister's well-being.

'I know you will, Luke,' he smiled. 'You're a good kid.'

An hour before noon Millard was drawing water from the stone well when he heard horsemen approaching. There were two of them. He watched them ride up and his heart sank as he recognized Jamie Lamont, whom he'd pole-axed in Reposo the previous afternoon. The other rider was Lew, Mr Lamont's foreman at the ranch. Jamie was scowling darkly, whereas the ranch foreman raised his hand in a natural, friendly salute.

'Stay where you are, Lew,' Jamie commanded the foreman, but then dismounted himself and turned to face the homesteader. Lew muttered something that Millard didn't catch.

'I'm telling you to keep out of it, Lew,' Jamie said angrily. 'I only asked you along to see there was fair play.'

The look of bewilderment on Lew's face indicated that everything that was happening was news to him. Meanwhile, Jamie Lamont had turned his attention back to the man at the well.

'You made a fool of me yesterday,' he snarled. 'In front of the whole town. And you got away with it because I was drunk and couldn't defend myself. Well, now I'm sober and I'm gonna teach you a lesson you won't forget.'

The ranch foreman watched them uneasily. Both men were wearing their gunbelts; he hoped that they could settle their differences with fisticuffs rather than resort to something more drastic. Millard looked much wearier than the last time they'd met, but Lew was a good judge of men and he could tell that the homesteader could look after himself.

But at that moment Millard was not thinking of himself. His thoughts were on Maggie and the baby; the last thing he wanted to do was to disturb or frighten them in any way.

'Listen,' he told the youngster facing him. 'I got a sick girl in the house. She's got a high fever and I cain't even leave her long enough to go looking for a doctor. What say we settle this some other time?'

Still seated in the saddle, Lew nodded his head in agreement but didn't dare say a word. Jamie was a headstrong youth who was likely to react badly to advice. For his part Jamie Lamont already felt he was getting the better of his adversary.

'You gonna fight me or not?' he demanded.

'Nope, I ain't,' Millard replied. 'But I am asking you to ride away and leave us in peace. We got enough problems as it is.'

Unfortunately, his plea fell on stony ground.

'You're yellow, mister,' Jamie told him. 'You're a yellow sonofabitch!'

Lew saw the colour drain from Millard's cheeks, but Jamie Lamont failed to see the warning signs. Confident of his ascendancy over the homesteader, the youngster let his hand drop to his holster.

'I'm calling you, mister,' he said tersely.

Jamie's gun had only just cleared the holster when he realized that Millard's Colt was levelled and aimed right between his eyes. Then Millard walked towards him and brought the barrel of the .45 to rest in the middle of his forehead. Jamie had let his own gun fall to the ground by now; he was shaking badly and the sweat of fear was running freely down his cheeks.

'Now you just get back on your horse and head back where you came from,' Millard said without raising his voice. 'If you ever draw on me again you're a dead man.'

The ranch foreman watched the youngster scramble into the saddle and ride away. He didn't attempt to follow him; he'd had enough of Jamie Lamont for one day.

'He hoodwinked me into coming with him,' he informed Millard. 'He ain't told anyone at the ranch about a fight in Reposo. I'm sure glad you went easy on him. You won't believe this, but he ain't such a bad young feller; he's going through a wild patch, that's all.'

Millard nodded his head sympathetically. Lew was a good man; he'd done everything right just now.

'You coming in for a coffee?' he asked the visitor. 'I reckon we both could do with one.'

'Sure thing,' Lew smiled. 'Then I'm gonna fix you up with some help; that's the least I can do.'

The ranch foreman was as good as his word. After assessing the needs of Maggie and the children he rode back to the Lamont ranch-house, only to reappear later in the afternoon driving a surrey and accompanied by a well-dressed lady with a pleasant smile on her face.

'That's the feller I was telling you about, Mrs Lamont,' Lew said as he brought the horses to a halt in the yard. Millard had come out of the house and was hurrying to help his lady visitor down from her seat.

'I was gonna bring the maid along,' Lew told the homesteader. 'But Mrs

Lamont insisted on coming over herself.'

'I'm mighty grateful to you, ma'am,' Millard said, removing his Stetson as he spoke. 'Maggie's more restful than she was, but she's pretty weak.'

'Can't I go inside and see her?' Mrs Lamont asked.

'Yeah . . . sure,' Millard stammered. 'Only I guess it ain't much of a place for a lady such as yourself to be visiting. I ain't had chance to tidy things up today.'

'I haven't always been a rancher's wife, Mr Millard,' she replied with a smile. 'Matt and myself lived as rough as the rest of them when we first settled here as young people. I guess we've been luckier than most, but it doesn't change the way we think.'

She made her way into the house and said hello to Luke, who was playing with Abigail in front of the fire.

'I've brought cookies for you,' she informed the boy. 'Why don't you go and help your pa unload the surrey?

You can leave your little sister with me. I'm not going to harm her.'

Maggie tried to rise from her sick-bed when she heard the stranger's voice, but the effort was still beyond her. However, her first glimpse of Mrs Lamont cuddling the baby in the doorway of the bedroom reassured her. The girl could tell instinctively that this was a good woman who meant them no harm.

'Have you eaten today, my girl?' the rancher's wife inquired. 'No? Well, I've brought you freshly baked pastries and some fruit to pick you up. You must need all your strength to hold this bonny baby for long. My, she weighs almost as much as me!'

Mrs Lamont spent over an hour at the homestead and the change in Maggie was remarkable. It was as if the comforting presence of another woman relieved her of all her worries concerning the family. Soon the girl was sitting up in bed, nibbling shyly at the treats the visitors had brought with them. Her brother Luke also took advantage of the occasion to eat quantities of the sweetmeats that were a rarity for him.

'I'm sure you're over the worst, Maggie,' Mrs Lamont assured the girl as she prepared to take her leave. 'But I've already sent word to Doctor Nelson in Reposo to call on you tomorrow morning. I'll be here about the same time as today. No, please don't protest; I'm sorry that you're ill, but at least it gives me something worthwhile to do now that my own son is all grown up.'

Jess Millard felt a flush of embarrassment rise to his cheeks at her words, but fortunately she didn't mention Jamie again. Meanwhile, Mrs Lamont was collecting the empty baskets which had recently been packed with foodstuff.

'As for Doctor Nelson,' the rancher's wife went on, 'he won't present you with a bill. That's all arranged. Tom and Amy were good neighbours and I can see how well you've been caring for

Abigail, so I'm only too pleased to help. By the way, you must visit us at the ranch when you're strong enough — all of you, I mean. It will give me a chance to try out my cooking. Now I'm not going to leave here till you promise that you'll come . . . '

It was getting dark when Lew finally got Mrs Lamont home to the ranch. As he unhitched the horses by the side of the stables he saw Jamie Lamont sauntering towards him. It was the first time he'd seen the young hothead since noon and he'd been hoping to avoid him for a little longer.

'Lew . . . '

'Yeah, Jamie?'

'I want to talk to you about what happened this morning.'

Lew suppressed a sigh. As if he didn't have enough to do keeping the cowpokes in line, recently he'd had to act as nursemaid to his boss's son, and keep his temper at the same time.

'Go ahead and talk, Jamie.'

The youngster hesitated; he seemed tongue-tied.

'I don't want you to say anything about it to the ranch-hands — about me backing down, I mean.'

The foreman stared at him. 'You didn't back down, Jamie,' he said. 'He had a gun pointed right at your head. There was nothing you could do about it, nor me either.'

Jamie Lamont fell silent for a few moments. His next statement took Lew by surprise. The ranch foreman was expecting to be blamed for not doing more to help his companion in his hour of need.

'I shouldn't have called him yellow, Lew,' Jamie said regretfully. 'I was in a temper and I said it without thinking it through. He ain't yellow, Lew, and nobody could have blamed him if he'd killed me for saying it.'

'He didn't want to kill you or anybody,' Lew said gently. 'He was just worried about his family, that's all.'

'I guess so,' Jamie said. 'I was wrong

there, too. He told me how things stood and I didn't want to hear him. I just wanted to get my own back.'

'Well, there's no real harm done,' Lew told him. 'Just be more careful in future. It would kill your ma if anything happened to you.'

'Yeah, you're right,' the youngster agreed. 'Thanks, Lew.'

The foreman watched the slim silhouette walk away into the deepening shadows that were enveloping the ranch buildings.

Maybe the kid's growing up at last, he thought with a wry smile.

13

As Jess Millard began to develop ideas of his own regarding the running of the homestead, he made more frequent journeys to Reposo where he could purchase the tools and materials he needed to turn his ideas into reality.

He nearly always travelled alone; although Maggie was over the worst of her illness, it had left her temporarily weakened and she preferred to devote what strength she had to the children and the house. Millard didn't much like leaving them alone, and he drilled into them the need to lock themselves indoors if any strangers approached while he was away. Fortunately the door was very sturdy and the windows had strong shutters. Anybody who risked smashing his way in would be an easy target for those inside the building.

'Don't worry what's happening outside,' Millard told Maggie and Luke. 'As long as you are all safe they can run off with the livestock if they like. Animals can always be replaced.'

Once he'd reached town Millard usually called in on one of the saloons to slake his thirst. He wasn't much of a drinker — drink had been the ruin of many a gunfighter — but a saloon was a good place to hear news and gossip after the isolation of the homestead; and sometimes the information picked up could prove useful.

Occasionally he ran into members of the Hollis gang who by now were a fixture in the township. People were wary of them but so far the outlaws hadn't put a foot wrong. Besides, Hollis and Marshal Reagan seemed to get on reassuringly well, and the citizens of Reposo were glad of that. Theirs was a nice town — dull and sleepy maybe but a good, safe place to live. Even Jamie Lamont and his two young cronies Mathew Stag and Victor Day had cooled down recently. They were still drinking at weekends but there was much less boisterousness and rowdyism than in the past.

Millard kept his distance from both groups, but observed them with an experienced eye. Jamie Lamont seemed embarrassed whenever he found himself in the same room as the homesteader and he was always anxious to whisk his two companions off to another watering-hole. As for the Hollis gang, they tended to keep themselves to themselves though Millard noticed that he seemed to take the interest of two of them: the blond-haired youngster he suspected of being involved in the shooting of the Lennoxes, and the swarthy member of the gang who was vaguely familiar to him. On more than one occasion he caught them watching him, though neither of them ever got round to talking to him.

Marshal Reagan's strategy was to keep on good terms with the outlaw gang for as long as they chose to remain in town. He drank every day with his old friend Hollis, and he was always civil to the rest of the bunch. In fact, many lawmen in the West would have approved of Reagan's tactics; any town marshal who believed in confrontation first was likely to end up in Boot Hill at an early age.

It was Reagan who informed Hollis that both Randall and Diego had spoken to him separately about Jess Millard.

'That feller Millard took over one of the homesteads a few weeks ago after Tom and Amy Lennox were shot dead,' Reagan said, and Hollis stiffened slightly in his chair. 'It's Millard himself who interests your Mexican friend, but Randall must have taken a liking to a girl Millard picked up here in town on his first visit. She's a dumb girl who blew in here with her kid brother a couple of years back. Nobody knows anything about their background, but Millard took a fancy to her and took her out to the homestead to look after

Tom and Amy's baby daughter.'

Hollis had become very pensive as he listened to the marshal's story. Randall had been showing signs of restlessness, and that could be dangerous. It might be best to get him out of town for a while and give him something to do. Franks and Bebb were quite content to play cards together to while away the time, but Hollis had noticed that whenever Randall joined them the game inevitably ended with an argument. Carling had hardly exchanged a civil word with Randall since Taylor's death; only Diego seemed to get on reasonably well with the youngster, and that was because the Mexican kept clear of gang squabbles.

'Is Millard's homestead on Double Q land?' Hollis asked suddenly.

'Nope,' the lawman replied. 'It's on Mr Lamont's range.'

'And is Quelch still looking for hands?'

'Only to look after the fences,' Reagan said.

'Yeah, that's what I mean,' Hollis remarked. 'Maybe I got a couple of men for him. I hope you can fix it up for me.'

It was easy for Marshal Reagan to get word to Quelch at the ranch that he'd like to meet him at the Red Sunset saloon on the following market day. The market was a monthly affair and most of the families living outside Reposo tried to make it there as a chance to socialize as well as barter and haggle over their wares.

Jess Millard also came into town that day, accompanied by young Luke who knew all the traders and enjoyed the hustle and bustle of the stalls and the mischievous pranks of the street urchins who'd been his friends for the last two years. Marshal Reagan was locking the jailhouse door prior to rendezvousing with Quelch and Hollis at the saloon when he saw Millard and Luke driving by on the buckboard.

'Millard,' he called out. 'You and me got some business.'

The lawman unlocked the door again as the homesteader pulled the buckboard over to the side of the roadway.

'Wait here, Luke,' Millard told the boy. 'I won't be long. Pull hard on the reins if she moves.'

Inside the jailhouse Reagan had opened a desk drawer and was counting out a sheaf of dollar bills. Millard stood in the doorway and waited for him to finish counting.

'Here's the hundred greenbacks I promised you,' the lawman said. 'The county sheriff took my word that the man we found was an outlaw, so let's keep our fingers crossed that he don't ever turn up alive someplace!'

Millard took the money with a polite nod of his head. He was wondering how much Reagan had made out of the transaction after he'd paid the undertaker's fees. The marshal was a bundle of tricks, a real wheeler and dealer. The homesteader didn't trust him an inch, but he returned the lawman's smile and kept his thoughts to himself. That was the best way to handle men like Reagan; let them think you couldn't see through them.

'I'm mighty grateful to you, Marshal,' he said. 'Especially since you did all the hard work . . . '

The town marshal beamed with happiness. He'd lined his own pocket and he'd also been generous enough to earn Millard's respect and gratitude. That was how he liked to operate — grease a palm here and there and build up a nice nest-egg for himself at the same time.

'I'd sure like to drink with you to celebrate our success,' he told his visitor, 'but I've got some important business to attend to at the Red Sunset; so if you'll excuse me . . . '

Hollis was lying on his bed on the first floor of the saloon when Franks came to inform him that the town marshal was asking for him downstairs.

'I'll be right down,' the gang leader said. He reached for his best velvet jacket and dusted it carefully. He wanted to make a good impression on the rancher.

Reagan was already seated at a table in a corner of the saloon together with a stocky, weatherbeaten man in his late forties. The bartender had set up three cold beers to help lubricate their deliberations. Hollis glanced around the room as he made his way among the tables. Carling and Bebb were at the counter, while Franks was cradling a whiskey glass at another table. Diego was standing just inside the doorway, his favourite vantage point.

The gang leader was irritated to find that Randall was missing. The clock on the wall behind the counter showed five minutes past noon, yet still the youngest member of the outlaw bunch hadn't showed. It didn't just irritate him; it made him angry.

'Let me introduce you two gentlemen' Reagan said with a fawning smile. 'Mr Quelch, Mr Hollis.'

The two men shook hands and Hollis sat down opposite the rancher.

'I guess the marshal's explained the situation to you,' Quelch said.

'He's told me what he knows,' the outlaw replied. 'But I'd like to hear it from you.'

'It's quite simple,' Quelch told him. 'A rancher called Lamont and myself share the range this side of the Pecos. The boundaries between his land and mine aren't always clearly defined, but we've never clashed over that. If his critters stray my cowpokes drive them back to his herd and his boys have always returned the favour. I may have the larger herd but Lamont was here before me, and I respect that.'

'If you and Lamont get on so well, what's the problem?' Hollis asked drily.

'Lamont's old-fashioned,' Quelch said. 'He lives in the past. Just because it's peaceful around here don't mean it's gonna stay that way for ever. You only got to read the newspapers to know there are cattle wars raging in other parts. I'm worried that one day we'll see herds from outside driven across our range, eating our grass, drinking our water and backed up by large outfits with plenty of fire-power. That's why I've started fencing off access to watering places so that I'll be able to patrol them with the number of men available to me.'

'So you're denying Lamont access to the river,' Hollis observed bluntly.

Quelch shook his head. 'Not at all,' he said. 'In fact I've urged him to do the same thing for his cattle, but he's short-sighted and he sees my fences as a threat.'

Hollis was disappointed by the reply. The outlaw leader thrived on conflict and violence. The man opposite him was too reasonable, too open and honest — the kind of man Hollis despised.

'Mr Quelch needs reliable fellers to protect his teams of fencers,' Reagan said.

'Well, I can spare you two good men for a start,' Hollis told the rancher. 'That's one of them over there by the door. You got any objection to Mexicans?'

'Nope, not if they're good men like you say,' Quelch replied. 'But I don't want anyone who's too trigger-happy neither.'

Hollis thought immediately of Randall. 'They ain't trigger-happy, Mr Quelch,' he lied, 'but they'll protect your cowpokes real good . . . '

In the meantime Jess Millard was picking his way among the market stalls with young Luke at his side. Millard was conscious that his pockets were bulging with money and he carefully avoided being jostled by passers-by. It occurred to him that a few weeks earlier he might have celebrated his good fortune by taking a shot at the gaming-tables or a card session with a saloon gambler. Now, however, he had responsibilities and he had no desire to risk his money like that. He resolved to give Luke a couple of dollars to treat himself and his friends to some candies. He'd have liked to buy something nice for Maggie, too, but it was years since he'd bought a girl a present and he didn't know where to begin looking.

Suddenly Luke pulled at his sleeve.

'What's up?' Millard inquired. 'You seen something you want?'

'There's a feller watching us, Jess,' the youngster informed him. 'He's standing under the barber's pole.'

Millard glanced casually around and saw Randall lolling in the shop doorway. The blond-haired outlaw didn't bother to avert his gaze, but just kept staring as if he wanted to provoke a confrontation. Normally Millard would have accepted the challenge, especially since he'd have liked to know how Randall had obtained the gun he'd later sold in Reposo. But now he had the boy with him, and he wanted to avoid trouble.

'D'you know him, Luke?' he asked, leading the kid off in the other direction.

'I seen him once before,' the

youngster replied. 'It was when you had the fight outside the coffee shop. He was there looking on, only he didn't help me and Maggie none.'

'Mr Millard . . . '

The homesteader half-turned and saw Mrs Lamont, the rancher's wife, coming towards them. To his dismay, she was accompanied by her son Jamie. When Jamie Lamont realized where she was heading he tried to hang back, but his mother grabbed his sleeve and pulled him along in her wake.

'I'm glad to see you, Mr Millard,' Mrs Lamont said with a smile that reflected her frank and genuine nature. 'Is Maggie still on the mend?'

Jess Millard was suddenly tongue-tied and Luke had to answer for him.

'She sure is, Mrs Lamont,' he piped up. 'She's eating better than I ever knowed her.'

'That's good,' the rancher's wife beamed. 'You men have got to make sure of that. She's just a slip of a girl, and she needs building-up.'

'We will,' Millard assured her earnestly. 'And I won't forget how you helped us out, Mrs Lamont.'

'Tut, tut; that was nothing,' she said. 'By the way, let me introduce you to my son Jamie. I was lucky enough to bump into him before he started on one of his sprees with his friends in town. He's a real tearaway — aren't you, Jamie?'

She ushered the red-faced youngster forward. There was an awkward moment as both men hesitated, but then Millard extended his hand and Jamie Lamont accepted it. Although the youngster averted his gaze as they shook hands, Millard guessed correctly that it was through embarrassment rather than resentment for what had happened between them.

'How are you off for money, Mr Millard?' the rancher's wife asked unexpectedly.

'Oh, pretty good,' Millard stammered. 'I got lucky just now.'

'I was thinking of Maggie,' Mrs Lamont explained. 'After an illness a girl often feels down, and a small present can help to raise her spirits.'

'I was thinking along the same lines myself,' he confessed. 'Only I ain't got any idea what to get her.'

'Well, let me see. Could you run to five dollars — ten maybe?'

'I can run to more than that, Mrs Lamont,' he assured her.

'Good,' she beamed. 'We'll go to Jackson's the goldsmith's. He always gives me a discount!'

Evening shadows were falling as the buckboard trundled down the slope leading to the homestead. Maggie had heard them coming and she came out into the yard to greet them. Little Luke leapt off the waggon before the wheels stopped turning and his sister gave him a warm hug.

'Maggie,' he said excitedly. 'Come and see all the candies Jess has bought.'

Millard was not far behind him. He handed the girl a small metal box and told her to open it. She did so and saw the gold locket and chain resting on a purple velvet cloth.

'It's for you, Maggie,' he said. 'It's for you to wear.'

She stared at the gift for a moment and then turned sharply and ran into the house. Then he could hear the sound of sobbing from inside the building. Motioning Luke to stay in the yard, Millard went into the house. Maggie was standing by the table, still holding the locket in her hand, the tears streaming down her cheeks.

'Maggie,' Millard told her. 'I didn't mean to upset you. God's truth I didn't.'

He walked over to the table and put his hand on her shoulder. She turned to face him, and then he did something crazy. He kissed her on the mouth and tasted the salt from her tears mingled with the sweetness of her lips.

She gave a little sigh and her body went limp. He thought she was going to faint; instead she clung on to him to steady herself. He kissed her again and again and she didn't pull away.

'I love you, Maggie,' he whispered. 'I want you to stay with me always.'

14

Randall and Diego arrived at the Double Q ranch in the late afternoon of the next day. Quelch had sent Bennet, his foreman, to Reposo to meet them and escort them to the ranch-house by a circuitous route that allowed them to get to know the lie of the land, the location of the fenced-off areas, and roughly where Quelch territory ended and Lamont domain began.

Diego and Bennet took to one another from the start. In his youth the ranch foreman had had a brief but torrid relationship with a Mexican girl he'd met in Laredo.

'She wanted me to marry her,' Bennet confided with a rueful grin. 'But I was too young. I'd only just started as a cattle drover and I just didn't have the money to settle down.'

Randall listened to their small-talk in

stony silence. When Hollis had first discussed sending the two of them to help Quelch, Randall had seen it as a chance to meet up with the girl he'd caught sight of in front of the coffee-shop. Then it became apparent that the homestead where she lived was out of bounds to Quelch's men since it was right in the middle of Lamont territory. Randall took the news badly, though he was careful to conceal his disappointment from the other outlaws. The less they knew about his feelings for the girl, the better.

When they reached the ranch, Bennet took them straight over to the bunkhouse which they were to share with the other cowboys.

'It gets pretty crowded in here at times,' he warned them. 'But there are two empty top bunks just inside the door. While you're settling in I'll go tell the cook there'll be two extra hands for supper.;

The Mexican clambered up onto the nearest spare bunk and stretched out. It felt good to be back on a ranch. It reminded him of his first job as a vaquero in his own country south of the border. He earned more money as a gunslinger, but sometimes he still hankered after the innocent days of his youth.

Meanwhile Randall had made his way deeper into the long room, and was making himself comfortable on one of the lower bunks that belonged to one of Quelch's cowpokes. Diego risked a glance over the edge of his bunk and saw that Randall had opened the hip-flask he always carried with him. It wasn't that the youngster was a heavy drinker, but he did like a swig of whiskey when he was feeling edgy. When Randall was feeling edgy he was also inclined to be dangerous, so Diego refrained from reminding him that he was occupying somebody else's bed.

The Mexican was just about dozing off when the bunkhouse door swung open and three trail-weary cowpokes walked stiffly into the room. The biggest of them was a man called Murphy; he made his way over to his bunk and stared in disbelief at the stranger lying there.

'You're in my place, feller,' he said gruffly. 'Go bed down elsewheres.'

'And you go to hell!' Randall told him, rolling over onto his side to face the wall.

Murphy was a man of few words and great strength. He took hold of the straw mattress in his huge hands and flicked it upwards. Randall was projected heavily against the wall, and when he rebounded Murphy contemptuously let the mattress fall onto his body. That was a mistake, because when Randall extricated himself from the mattress his Colt was already in his hand.

Murphy froze as Randall rose to his feet. The gunslinger took advantage of the big feller's paralysis to move in swiftly and bring the butt of the .45 down hard on the man's skull. Murphy staggered and reached for one of the bunk props to support himself. Then Randall dealt him a savage blow on the side of the face that opened a deep gash in his cheek.

Murphy sank to his knees, groaning and trying to stem the flow of blood with the palm of his hand. Randall raked his two companions with a disdainful glance.

'Now d'you understand?' he challenged them. 'I didn't come here to get pushed around!'

The mood among the Double Q hands changed quickly as soon as the word spread that Randall was unpredictable and dangerous.

'I'd feel a lot safer with a scorpion in my sleeping-bag than with that feller Randall in the bunkhouse,' was how one cowhand put it to Bennet the foreman when the gunslinger was safely out of hearing. 'Usually it's greaseballs I don't get on with, but Diego's an angel compared with that other feller.'

'You want to keep an eye on both of them,' another cowboy chimed in.

'There's no telling what trouble they'll stir up if they ain't kept on a tight rein.'

Bennet shrugged his shoulders philosophically. 'That's Mr Quelch's problem,' he replied. 'But if I was Lamont's boys, I'd keep well away from our fencing in future.'

The first job the two gunmen were given was to escort a waggon carrying wire to a team of men working near a branch of the main river. The waggon was driven by a toothless old-timer called Henry who chewed tobacco incessantly so that his bearded chin was stained black by the stuff.

The route took them past some hilly, rocky terrain. Henry turned out to be the sort of driver who can spot a jack-rabbit a mile off while still concentrating on the next bump in the road ahead.

'Them Lamont boys don't miss a trick,' he yelled suddenly to the two gunslingers who were riding on either flank of the clattering waggon.

Randall jerked his head around and

scanned the horizon. As usual he was in the mood for trouble.

'Where's that?' he demanded. 'I don't see nothing.'

'Just under the ridge,' the old-timer said. 'Two of 'em. They don't mean no harm. They're just curious where the next fence is going so's they can tear it down again when nobody's looking.'

'I see them,' Diego said. He glanced over at Randall, whose face was inscrutable. It was only when they'd passed out of sight of the ridge that the young outlaw suddenly swung his mount away from the waggon.

'Let's go see what they're up to,' he told the Mexican. 'They won't be expecting us to pay them a visit.'

They rode in a wide arc to approach the ridge from another direction. Diego would have preferred to stay with the waggon but he felt obliged to keep an eye on his unstable pardner.

They approached the ridge from out of the sun and so were unobserved. At last they caught sight of the Lamont cowhands walking their horses casually away from Double Q land. Randall drew his carbine from its scabbard; the range was only a few hundred yards.

'What are you gonna do?' Diego asked tersely.

'Nothing; just scare them, that's all.'

His shot echoed among the rocks. One of the riders twisted and struggled for a few moments until his mount collapsed under him and rolled over on its side, forcing him to jump clear. Randall's slug had wounded the animal fatally. Diego expected the cowboys to return the fire. Instead, they sought the shelter of some neighbouring rocks, taking the surviving horse with them.

'Well, at least they won't be able to come after us,' Randall remarked with a cold smile. 'Let's get back to the waggon.'

15

When Matt Lamont was informed that two of his cowpokes had been attacked without provocation, he despatched Lew, his foreman, to the Double Q ranch-house to demand to know what was going on. Quelch was just as surprised as Lamont had been by the news Lew brought him. The two gunslingers hadn't even reported the incident to him.

Lamont's choice of emissary was a good one: Quelch respected Lew as an honest, well-meaning man. He promised the foreman that he'd look into the matter and warn his cowboys not to be so gun-happy in future. In reply Lew told him that Lamont had already instructed his men to keep to their own territory except when they were legitimately rounding up stray cattle. Neither rancher wanted open warfare. Quelch knew he held the upper hand at the moment, but what if Lamont decided to go looking for gunslingers of his own? If they didn't tread carefully the situation could get out of control.

When Lew had departed Quelch told his own ranch foreman Bennet to bring the two hired guns to see him as soon as they got back. When Bennet ushered them into the rancher's study a few hours later, Diego let Randall do all the talking. True to character, Randall expressed no regret for opening fire on the Lamont cowhands.

'They were on Double Q land,' he told the rancher. 'Your waggon driver told us they were up to no good, so me and Diego thought we'd put a scare into them. I don't see there was any harm done.'

Quelch pursed his lips but felt that he couldn't reprimand the men's actions. They'd been brought in to protect his interests and that's what Randall obviously believed they'd been doing.

'Yeah, well . . . OK,' he conceded. 'At

least Lamont's promised to keep his men away from my enclosures for the time being. I think you boys should go back to Reposo for a few days until I need you.'

Randall fixed him with a cold stare. 'Does that mean you're paying us off,' he inquired, 'just for looking after your interests?'

'No ... no, not at all,' Quelch stammered. 'You'll be fully paid while I think what job to give you next. There's always plenty to do on a ranch.'

'That's fine then,' Randall said with a thin smile. 'We'll be ready anytime. You know where to find us.'

★   ★   ★

Hollis and the rest of the gang weren't expecting them back so soon. Their account of ranch politics set the gang leader thinking. Till now he'd only thought of Reposo as a backwater to rest up in. In fact the township was set bang in the middle of rich pasture land where inter-ranch rivalries might boil over at any time. These were conditions in which the Hollis gang could thrive, especially since Reposo had a lazy, acquiescent marshal, which made it a natural refuge for the outlaws if things started to go wrong.

Now that Randall was idle again, Hollis told Diego to keep an eye on him. The outlook was promising in the sleepy township, he didn't want the youngster screwing things up. Diego didn't enjoy the show of friendship he had to put on for Randall's benefit, but he respected his leader's judgement. The gang had to hold together to prosper and they all realized that Randall's lack of self-control was the weak link in the chain.

The Mexican sensed that something was up one day around noon. Randall had been lounging by the window of the Red Sunset saloon when he stiffened suddenly in his chair and craned his neck to get a better view of what was going on outside. The

Mexican's eye followed his gaze. The only novelty he could see was the arrival in the main street of a buckboard driven by the homesteader Jess Millard.

He glanced again at Randall; the young gunslinger had risen to his feet and was making for the swing-doors leading out to the street. Diego watched him walk swiftly towards the stable where the gang kept their horses. A few minutes elapsed and then Randall reappeared, mounted on his nutbrown pony. Diego saw Jess Millard enter the hardware store a hundred yards away. Was it coincidence that Randall was riding out just as the homesteader arrived? The Mexican decided to find out. After all, that was what Hollis had told him to do.

Randall had a few minutes start but that suited Diego's purpose. He could easily follow the younger man from a distance without being spotted. It didn't take him long to conclude that Randall wasn't heading for the Double

Q ranch. He was heading for Lamont territory, and in particular the trail that led to the homestead where Millard and the young girl lived.

When the Mexican was certain of Randall's destination he spurred his mount into a gallop and caught up with the youngster in a matter of minutes. Randall reined in the pony as Diego rode up close; he seemed none too pleased to see him.

'I saw you ride out of town and thought you might like company,' the Mexican said affably. 'Where are you heading?'

'Just visiting an old friend,' Randall replied curtly. 'And I don't need no company.'

Sensing hostility in the young gun-slinger's voice, Diego resorted to diplomacy.

''Tain't nothing to do with me,' he said, 'but Mr Quelch warned us to keep away from Lamont land. Hollis don't want us to upset Quelch, not while he's paying our wages.'

'That's all you're good for,' Randall told him contemptuously. 'Running errands for Hollis.'

'Hollis don't even know I followed you,' the Mexican said. 'I just don't want you and him to fall out, that's all.'

Diego had made a fatal mistake. Randall began to think quickly.

'Go tell Hollis I ain't falling out with him nor anybody,' he said. 'But I gotta see this girl, and the Devil himself ain't gonna stop me.'

The Mexican had other ideas about that: Jess Millard had helped him out once. He wasn't going to let Randall harm his woman. The time for talking was past.

Both men went for their guns simultaneously, but Randall was in a different class. He fired from close range and the pain and shock registered on Diego's face as the slug smashed his shoulder and paralysed his shooting arm. Randall fired again, almost point-blank into the Mexican's chest. Diego slumped forward in the saddle, his eyes glazed in death.

Randall re-holstered his Colt with a growing sense of elation. His day was just beginning.

*   *   *

'Maggie!'

The girl turned from the washing tub to see what her young brother wanted. The boy's face was grubby and Maggie smiled as she made circular movements with her hand to indicate that he should give it a scrub. Luke merely shrugged the suggestion aside.

'I'm going to the woods,' he told her. 'Jesse ain't had no time to stock up with firewood today. I'll wash my face when I get back,' he added as an after-thought, then ran off out into the yard before his sister could protest.

Randall watched the boy's progress from the shelter of a cottonwood grove where he'd tethered the pony. With the kid out of the way he could concentrate on surprising the girl. He moved stealthily, keeping the sun behind him and using the cover of the scattered farm buildings whenever he could. He reached the house without incident and found the door wide open. He stepped into the shaded coolness of the interior. The girl was standing a few yards away, staring out of the window towards the woods to make sure that her young brother was safe.

She turned suddenly as if she could sense the presence of a stranger in the room. Randall grinned at her lecherously and the colour drained from her slim face. She started to make for the other room but the gunslinger was too quick for her. He pushed her against the heavy oak table and bent her back over it. He pressed his body against hers and she felt the stubble of his beard on her cheek.

'It's been a long time, Maggie,' he told her. 'You were no more than fourteen then, remember?'

She was trying to push him away but her illness had drained her of all her strength. When he spoke his voice was a mixture of lust and venom.

'I almost had you then, Maggie, like I'm gonna have you now. Only you called out for help and that fool father of yours came and tried to pull me off you. Then I killed him, but it took me long enough for you to get away. Is that what struck you dumb, Maggie — getting your pa killed like that? Well, I guess you ain't gonna yell out this time, so nobody's gonna get hurt.'

He wrapped his arms around her and dragged her struggling into the next room. She was gasping with fright but he forced her down onto the bed and began tearing the clothes from her body. When she was half-naked he began working on his own clothing. His breath was also coming in gasps, but for a different reason. He was pressing his body weight down upon her but she managed to raise her head an instant. Her eyes opened wide and her cheeks turned purple as her lips struggled to make a sound.

'Luke . . . Luke. Get away . . . Run!'

It was the first time her brother had heard her say a word in years, yet he didn't heed her supplication. He'd forgotten the knife, the one Jess Millard had bought him, and he'd come back for it. He was holding it in his small hand and he brought it down as hard as he could onto the back of the gunslinger's thigh.

'Aaah . . . ' Randall screamed with pain and rolled over onto the floor clutching his injured leg. In a flash the girl was on her feet and was whisking the baby up from the crib. Then Maggie and Luke raced out of the house and into the yard, and made for the safety of the woods.

By the time Randall had managed to hobble over to the door they were already beyond accurate firing range. The gunslinger's face was contorted with rage.

'I'll be back for you, you bitch,' he yelled. 'And if you tell anybody about me you're dead. You're all dead!'

But now he had other things to worry about. He needed a length of cloth or linen to bandage his wound, and then he needed to put distance between himself and the homestead. The day which had started so well for him had suddenly turned sour.

16

Hollis was not unduly concerned about Randall and the Mexican's whereabouts for the next few hours. He inquired vaguely about them towards late afternoon, but Franks and Bebb merely shrugged their shoulders.

'If Randall was up to any mischief in town we'd have heard of it by now,' Carling remarked drily. 'And I don't want to waste any time looking for him. The less I see of him, the more I like it.'

'Wherever he is, Diego ain't far away,' Hollis said. 'I told the Mex to keep an eye on him.'

Franks and Bebb went on studying their cards. They shared Carling's opinion of the youngest member of the gang, and weren't going to let him spoil their game.

By midnight Hollis was frankly puzzled. He and Marshal Reagan had taken a drink in every saloon and bar in Reposo's main street and hadn't caught sight of the missing outlaws in any of them.

'Don't worry. They'll turn up,' the lawman said as they parted company outside the jailhouse. 'Maybe Quelch needed them and called them back to the Double Q in a hurry.'

'Yeah, maybe,' Hollis replied half-heartedly. He knew Diego pretty well and didn't think the Mexican would leave town without letting him know.

The gang leader was woken next morning by a loud knocking on his hotel-room door. His head was thick from the night before, but he had the presence of mind to pick up his Colt on his way to answer it.

'Oh, it's you, Bebb,' he muttered. 'Everything OK?'

'It's Randall,' Bebb informed him. 'He just got back. He's downstairs.'

Hollis stared at him. 'Where's the sonofabitch been all night?' he asked. 'Whoring?'

'Nope, walking. Someone shot his horse from under him yesterday and he had to walk most of the way back before a buckboard picked him up this morning.'

The gang leader hurried to get dressed and get downstairs. Randall was sitting in front of a bottle of whiskey, looking pretty sorry for himself.

'What happened?' Hollis asked him. 'Where's Diego?'

'I got bushwhacked,' Randall said sullenly. 'Happened about ten miles out of town. They came at me out of the sun — a bunch of them. I heard a shot and my horse went from under me, I got thrown and I hurt my leg. I thought I was a goner when I heard one of them yell something about teaching me a lesson. Then they all rode off and left me lying there.'

Hollis scratched his chin. There was no need to ask who the attackers were. The remark about teaching Randall a lesson could only point in one direction: Lamont. Despite the truce the two ranchers had declared Lamont's ranch-hands were clearly not in the mood to forgive and forget.

'I thought Quelch and Lamont had struck a deal,' Carling remarked from his vantage point at the window.

'Yeah, so did I,' Randall said ruefully.

'Where's the Mexican?' Hollis asked again. 'We ain't seen him since yesterday. Did he ride out with you?'

'Nope,' the youngster lied. 'Why should he: I just felt like stretching the pony's legs. Last I saw of Diego he was right here in this room.'

Hollis didn't like the sound of that. Diego had probably heeded his orders and followed Randall from a distance. If so, why hadn't he lent a hand when Randall came under attack? Had Diego also been bushwhacked by Lamont's cowhands? Uneasy, Hollis dispatched Franks and Bebb to the Double Q ranch-house to give Quelch the bad news and to inquire if anyone had seen the

Mexican or knew of his whereabouts.

The two outlaws returned to Reposo a few hours later, no wiser than when they'd departed.

'Quelch didn't believe us at first,' Franks told Hollis when the gang were gathered in an upstairs room of the Red Sunset. 'He said it wasn't like Lamont to break his word.'

'Maybe I dreamt it all,' Randall remarked bitterly. 'Maybe I shot my own horse from under me.'

'Calm down,' Hollis warned him. 'We gotta know where we stand. If we cain't rely on Quelch, we'll sort it out ourselves. Let's wait till we hear from Diego. In the meantime, Randall, you stick close to the saloon and don't take any risks.'

In the late afternoon four horsemen rode into Reposo and made straight for the marshal's office. The four men worked the Lamont spread — Lew the foreman, Martin an old-timer, and two younger cowboys Raikes and Williams. There was a fifth horse, with a dead man strapped to it. When Reagan went out to examine the corpse he recognized it at once.

'It's that Mexican feller,' he said. 'He went missing yesterday.'

'We found him on Lamont land,' Lew told him. 'He'd been shot twice. The horse had wandered a few hundred yards away to a watering hole.'

The lawman chewed on his cheroot. He didn't like this development. He decided not to mention Diego's connection with the Double Q. Lew seemed to know no more about the matter than what he'd said, and Reagan knew him to be an honest man. The lawman wasn't looking forward to breaking the news to Hollis and his gang — not one bit.

'Ain't no need for you boys to hang around, Lew,' he told the ranch foreman. 'The town will bury him as usual.'

Lew nodded his head. 'Thanks, Marshal,' he replied. 'We'll be getting along.'

As the four cowpokes rode slowly back through the township's main street, the two younger members of the group showed signs of restlessness.

'Goddamnit, Lew,' Williams said suddenly. 'I don't want to leave town without taking a drink, and neither does Raikes.'

''Tain't right, Lew,' Martin the old-timer chimed in. 'We oughta drink to that poor dead feller's soul. It's a Christian duty.'

The foreman nodded his head; it wasn't every day that the cowhands found themselves in the vicinity of a saloon.

'You go ahead,' he told the others. 'But count me out. I gotta get back and tell Mr Lamont.'

An hour later Hollis was summoned to the undertaker's parlour to identify the Mexican's body. Reagan was there waiting for him, anxious to explain what he knew about the killing. The lawman had the right to ask Hollis to pay for the burial, but the marshal's courage didn't run to that.

'I reckon them cowpokes was telling the truth,' Reagan said earnestly. 'I reckon he was bushwhacked by somebody who was just passing through.'

'Yeah, just like Randall,' Hollis snarled. 'Lamont's gonna pay for this, Reagan . . . '

There was no way that the town marshal could relax after the day's events. He sat in his office for a while, racking his brain to find a solution to the problem. His stay in Reposo had been congenial up till now; he was an easy-going lawkeeper and his experience and skill with a gun was adequate for most situations that arose in the sleepy township. Yet here he was, faced with an impending showdown between Lamont's ranch-hands and Hollis's gunslingers. He didn't like it one bit.

His hand was trembling as he locked the jailhouse door behind him and made for the nearest saloon. He needed a drink and some company to steady his nerves. Normally the Red Sunset was his favourite venue but he'd had enough of Hollis and his gang for one day. The tinkling of a honkytonk piano issued from the interior of the Western Trail hotel. The lawman pushed the swing doors open and went inside.

It came as an unpleasant surprise to him to see Martin, Williams and Raikes standing at the counter sharing a bottle of spirits. He'd assumed that they'd be back on Lamont territory by now. He strode over to the counter and ordered a whiskey. His voice sounded hoarse and he was conscious that his heart was thumping faster than usual. The bartender poured him a stiff drink that he downed in one gulp.

'You boys ain't planning to stay here all night, are you?' he asked the cowboys. 'Ain't Mr Lamont expecting you back?'

'Nice of you to be concerned, Marshal,' Martin said, slurring his words slightly. 'But it's a clear night and the horses know their way home even if we don't.'

Before the lawman could reply the doors of the saloon swung open again and Hollis walked in, accompanied by Franks, Bebb and Carling. The newcomers stared around the room in a challenging manner, and the piano playing faltered and then stopped altogether.

The gang leader's eye settled on the group of men standing at the bar. Apart from Reagan they were all strangers to him, but he noticed how the marshal's face had flushed and how Reagan had begun to move surreptitiously away from the other three fellers as if he didn't want to be associated with them. Hollis guessed at once who the men were, and so did the rest of the gunslingers who immediately took up strategic positions in the room so as not to be bunched up in case of gunplay. Meanwhile, the dozen or so customers had frozen in their chairs; only the three cowboys at the counter seemed oblivious to the atmosphere building up in the saloon.

At last Hollis addressed them directly.

'D'you boys work for Lamont?' he inquired.

Martin half-turned to face him. 'That's right, mister,' he conceded. 'Anything we can do for you?'

'I guess not. Not unless you can raise the dead.'

The three cowboys exchanged puzzled glances, they'd drunk too much to grasp subtleties.

'Now listen, Hollis,' the town marshal chimed in. 'There ain't no call . . . '

'Shut your trap, Reagan,' Hollis warned him. 'Keep out of this.'

The lawman's face turned even redder. Martin looked to him for some support, but Reagan's nerve had gone completely. The old-timer pushed his glass away contemptuously.

'I don't understand any of this,' he said. 'Let's get going, boys.'

'Stay where you are,' Hollis ordered, but Martin ignored him and made for the swing-doors. He'd taken about five steps when Hollis drew his Colt and shot him in the stomach. Incensed by his action Raikes and Williams went for their guns but were caught in a lethal crossfire from the other outlaws. When the shooting stopped all three of Lamont's cowhands were lying dead on the saloon floor.

Hollis realized suddenly that Reagan was already through the swing doors and outside in the street. The gang leader walked unhurriedly to the door to check on where the lawman was heading. As he pushed the flaps apart he noticed an object lying in the dust just outside the saloon. It was Reagan's badge of office; the lawman had had enough and was running away again.

Reagan had forty yards start on him, but then Hollis saw Randall limping along the sidewalk near the Red Sunset.

'It's Reagan,' he called out to the youngster, and pointed with his hand. 'Don't let him get away. Stop him!'

Pursuer and pursued disappeared into the shadows of the sidewalk. Then, a few moments later, Hollis heard a shot. As usual, Randall had carried out orders in the only way he knew.

17

Jess Millard's initial elation on learning that Maggie had recovered her power of speech was gradually tempered by the personality change that the miracle had brought with it. All the progress their relationship had made over the weeks was wiped out at a stroke. Maggie was once again wary of him, and avoided his touch; she was edgy and jumpy, unable to relax. Instead, she kept busy all her waking hours until Millard feared that the girl would collapse with exhaustion.

Strangely, Luke's attitude towards him had changed as well. The boy had come to enjoy helping Millard in the yard, the corral, the woods. But now he preferred to stick near the house, and seemed unwilling to let his sister out of his sight.

Jess Millard couldn't figure either of

them out. If he'd done something to upset them he was willing to rectify it. But when he tried to broach the subject they merely averted their gaze and went on with whatever they were doing.

When Lamont's foreman, Lew, rode up to the homestead one afternoon, Millard was glad to see him. They didn't get many visitors and maybe the novelty would draw Maggie and Luke out of themselves for a while.

While Maggie prepared a jug of coffee and her brother loitered by the window, Lew related his disturbing tale of violence.

'Three of our men were gunned down in Reposo the other night,' he told Millard. 'They'd taken in a dead body they'd found on our range. He was a Mexican and it seems he belonged to a gang of hoodlums who hole up in the Red Sunset saloon.'

Millard nodded his head. 'I know them,' he said. 'At least, I know them by sight.'

'Seems they got the wrong end of the

163

stick,' Lew went on. 'I was with our boys when we handed the body over to the marshal, but then I left them in town to do some drinking. Later on the Mexican's compadres caught up with them and killed them in cold blood.'

The girl carried the jug of steaming coffee over to the table and began pouring.

'What's the town marshal doing about it?' Millard asked.

'Nothing,' Lew replied. 'Reagan's dead too. That blond feller, Randall, shot him as he was trying to leave town. Reagan wasn't the sort who'd fight against the odds, but they got him just the same.'

The ranch foreman moved his arm sharply as hot coffee spilt onto the table. Millard glanced up and saw that the girl's hand was shaking violently. He took the jug from her in case she scalded herself.

'Are you OK, Maggie?' he inquired. 'You ain't falling sick again, are you?'

She shook her head and mumbled

something inaudible. She went and sat down near the fire and young Luke went to join her there. They both looked very pale.

'Quelch has been to see Mr Lamont,' Lew said. 'He don't want no part of it, though he admits he employed the Mexican and the blond feller to guard his fencing. All that's over now, though; Quelch has promised to side with us if there's any more trouble.'

'Will there be?' Millard asked.

'Not from our side,' Lew replied almost regretfully. 'We ain't no match for the Hollis gang. They're all of them killers. Trouble is, Jamie Lamont has taken it harder than anyone on the ranch. One of the men they killed was an old-timer who was good to Jamie when he was just a kid. We're all fearful that Jamie may take the law into his own hands and end up in Boot Hill himself . . . '

That night Millard was dozing fitfully in the barn when he felt someone tugging his arm. In the moonlight that streamed through the window he could see that it was Luke. The youngster's eyes were red and swollen with tears.

'What's wrong, Luke?' he asked. 'For God's sake, what's wrong?'

'I had a bad dream, Jess,' the boy blurted out. 'I dreamt he was coming back for me and Maggie and that he was gonna kill you.'

'Who was coming back? Who are you talking about?'

He put his arm around the boy's shoulders to stop his body shaking. Luke's willpower was all used up. Despite what his sister had told him, he had to let Millard know what had happened. He told everything he knew and it was enough for Millard to understand the nightmare Maggie had endured in silence.

'You go back to your sister now,' Millard said when Luke had finished speaking. 'Everything's gonna be OK.'

When he'd gone Millard rolled a smoke and pondered over what he should do. So Randall had threatened to return to the homestead. Well, he wouldn't wait for that to happen. He'd go to Reposo. He'd go to Reposo and tear the evil out by the root.

18

Jamie Lamont was unable to keep away from Reposo after the murder of the old-timer Martin and the other two ranch-hands. The killings had made Jamie grow up overnight. He no longer handed his gun over when he went into a saloon, and neither did his friends Mathew Stag and Victor Day. They whiled their time away in the Western Trail hotel where the floorboards were still stained with blood. They drank very little. Jamie Lamont knew that it would be crazy to walk into the Red Sunset and demand a showdown, so he determined to sit tight and see how things worked out.

The township was very subdued after the killing of the marshal. Feelings were running high, but nobody had the courage to act upon them. Everybody was surprised that the outlaw gang hadn't quit the town; but that wasn't Hollis's style.

'We ain't running,' he told his men. 'That way they'd think we were scared and they'd come after us. We'll bide our time and leave when we're ready. Besides, if Lamont gets round to blaming Quelch for what's happened, there could still be work for us in these parts.'

It was Victor Day who spotted Jess Millard as the homesteader rode past the Western Trail hotel in the direction of the saloon where Hollis and the others were holed up. When he called out the news, Jamie Lamont went to join him at the window.

'Heck, he must have heard about the shootings, but he's stopped outside the Sunset,' Day said. 'What if them gunslingers think he's one of your father's hands, Jamie?'

'I don't know,' Jamie replied. 'But I'm gonna follow him. Are you two coming?'

From his upstairs room Randall

watched Jess Millard heading for the saloon. Maybe it was a coincidence, or maybe the girl had talked. Either way Randall saw no point in hanging around for Millard to catch up with him. There was an external staircase leading to the back of the saloon. This was as good an opportunity as any to pay Maggie another visit.

Millard pushed the swing doors apart and glanced around the room. Carling was standing at the bar while Franks and Bebb were playing cards at a table near the centre of the room. Hollis and Randall were nowhere to be seen; he decided to have a drink at the counter until either or both of them showed up.

There were only a handful of customers at the table: a few drunks clustered near the piano and Big Ned, the chop-house proprietor, who was sharing a bottle with a local business-man. Ned nodded almost imperceptibly to Millard when their eyes met; the big man still shuddered with embarrass-ment at the memory of their first meeting, but he'd heard that Maggie was happy on the homestead and Ned was generous enough to feel glad for them both.

Millard turned sharply as the doors swung open behind him; but it wasn't the missing gunslingers. Jamie Lamont and his two companions sat down at the first table they came to and called out for three cold beers. When the bartender had carried their drinks over to them he returned to the counter. Millard also asked for beer and proceeded to sip it very slowly. All the time the bartender's face was impassive, but the man was experienced enough to detect the tension in the air.

Meanwhile, Millard refrained from glancing at Jamie Lamont or acknowledging him in any way. He didn't want to suck Jamie and his friends into any play he might decide to make.

Four or five minutes passed, and then Hollis descended the carpeted staircase. He'd just taken a bath and his skin looked shiny and healthy. He was still fastening the buckle of his gunbelt when he reached the bottom step.

'Where's Randall?' he asked in a loud voice as if everybody in the room was his servant. Carling, the nearest man to him, merely shrugged his shoulders.

'Still upstairs, I guess,' he replied.

Jess Millard moved a few feet away from the bar so that Carling no longer obscured his view of the gang leader.

'Tell him to come on down,' Millard said. 'I want a word with him.'

Hollis started at him; the outlaw wasn't used to taking orders from homesteaders. He felt his temper rising.

'Randall tried to violate my woman,' Millard went on. 'I don't like that. No feller would.'

Hollis's eyes narrowed. 'Listen, amigo,' he said coldly. 'Randall has violated lots of women, and he's killed lots of men. Just go back where you came from, and be glad you're still alive to enjoy your woman even if she is Randall's leftovers!'

There was a clatter of furniture as

Big Ned jumped to his feet. He hadn't always been as kind to Maggie as he felt he should have, especially in drink, but he'd been the only man in Reposo to offer her a job when she needed it, and the girl had worked hard for him in return. Nobody was going to talk about her like that, as if she was a common whore.

'You bad-mouthing sonofabitch,' he snarled, and Hollis swung round to meet the new threat. Ned was close enough to seize hold of Hollis but stupidly he reached for a chair, intending to inflict as much damage as he could. Hollis took a step backwards, drew his Colt and pumped a bullet into Ned's body. The big man roared with pain and rage and then sank to his knees with blood spouting from his lips.

Carling hadn't taken his eyes off Jess Millard, the one who'd caused all the trouble. Millard stared back at him, his eyes full of challenge. Carling was not the sort of feller to resist a challenge like that, not when Bebb and Franks had got to their feet and were ready to back him up.

Carling's hand fell onto the butt of his .45, but compared to Millard the gunslinger was a novice. The homesteader's Colt barked once and the slug flattened Carling's chest against the counter. Millard didn't waste a further bullet on him. Carling's life had only a few moments to run.

As Franks and Bebb drew their guns Jamie Lamont leapt to his feet, followed closely by Victor Day. Jamie had already slid his gun from its holster under the cover of the table. He aimed vaguely in the direction of the two outlaws and pulled the trigger; a whiskey bottle disintegrated a few inches from Bebb's hip. The two gunslingers hadn't anticipated this intervention and they spun round to deal with it. Victor Day and Bebb fired almost simultaneously. Day's shot missed Bebb completely but caught Franks in the midriff and doubled him up like a jack-knife. Bebb was more accurate; his slug smashed into Day's shoulder and threw the youngster backwards. Then Bebb made for the swing doors, throwing a shower of lead at Jamie Lamont and Mathew Stag, who immediately scattered and sought cover behind the furniture.

Meanwhile, Hollis was edging his way slowly up the staircase, hoping that Randall would show up and give him backing. Millard had flattened himself against the counter, behind Carling's body; there he was fairly safe from the bullets Hollis was sending his way, but it wasn't the best of positions to get in an accurate shot of his own. Then he saw the gang leader stumble and fall backwards onto the stairs. Had he lost his footing, had he been hit, or was he bluffing? The homesteader didn't hesitate; he left the safety of the counter and ran to the foot of the stairs. Hollis righted himself enough to loose off another shot, and Millard felt the slug tear the skin away from his left side. He fired back, aiming for his adversary's chest but the slug went high and a hole opened up in the middle of the outlaw's temple. Hollis sagged and his head fell back onto the staircase, his eyes staring vacantly at the ceiling of the floor above.

Jamie Lamont realized he was hit when his right leg received what felt like a kick from a mule. He held on to a table top to stop himself falling, but he was helpless to do anything as Bebb rushed past him on the way out into the street. Jamie stared at Mathew Stag, who hadn't even drawn his gun yet. Stag's face was white with fear and shock.

'Do something, you yeller sonofabitch,' Jamie yelled through gritted teeth. 'Do something!'

Like a zombie Stag drew his gun and walked out through the swing-doors. Bebb was busy untethering the nearest horse at the rail outside the saloon. The moving shadow of the doors told him he'd been followed. Instinctively, the outlaw raised his Colt, aimed it at Mathew Stag and pulled the trigger.

The hammer came down on an empty chamber. Then the youngster raised his own weapon and fired into the outlaw's chest at point-blank range. The horse shied away as Bebb fell against it and onto the ground.

A handful of spectators had gathered at the sound of the shooting. Strangely, some of them started to clap their hands, and one of them shouted, 'Well done, Mathew.'

The youngster couldn't see them. His eyes were full of tears. He turned away from the dead man, leaned on the hitching-rail and began to retch violently.

19

When Millard had searched the hotel thoroughly and was certain that Randall had made his getaway, he knew that he must return at once to the homestead. He thought it unlikely that the outlaw would make his way there since it was on Lamont territory. Randall was probably high-tailing it in the opposite direction by now, but he had threatened Maggie and the boy, and Jess Millard didn't want to take any risks as far as they were concerned.

The town doctor had arrived and was tending the wounded. There was nothing Millard could do to help so he pushed his way through the throng of townsfolk who'd gathered in and around the Red Sunset saloon now that the shooting was over.

He rode back to the homestead as

quickly as was possible without exposing the gelding to the risk of stumbling in the poor light. When he finally reached the farm he was relieved to see its windows shuttered and its solid door closed firmly. He dismounted by the corral and led his mount over to the barn. The door creaked as he pulled it open. As he turned again to lead the horse inside he was struck suddenly by a heavy blow to the side of the head and felt himself slipping into oblivion.

His head ached with a sickening pain when Randall threw a pail of cold water into his face to bring him round. Millard groaned and tried to bring his hands up to his head, then realized that they were securely tied behind his back.

'Listen, you sonofabitch, and listen good,' Randall said tersely. 'I'm gonna help you up and then we're gonna walk over to the house. You're gonna call out to the girl to let you in. But remember this, if you let on that you ain't alone I'll kill you and I'll burn the house down with Maggie and the kids inside.

If you're sensible I'll be gone in an hour and you'll all live to tell the tale.'

Even with the gunslinger's help Millard could hardly make it to his feet. Randall half-dragged, half-carried him across the yard to the door of the homestead. When they reached it Randall had to use both his arms to keep Millard upright.

'Call out,' he hissed into the home-steader's ear. 'Call out or you're all dead.'

Millard was too ill to protest. He called Maggie's name hoarsely and then repeated it with as much strength as he could muster.

'I'm coming, Jess. I'll unbolt the door.'

Randall grinned malevolently as he heard the bar being drawn. As the door slackened he pushed Millard to the ground and kicked hard at the wood-work. The heavy door flew open and hurled Luke half-way across the room. Randall looked around and saw Maggie standing near the window. She was holding a gun in her hands, the gun that had once belonged to his fellow outlaw Taylor.

Randall froze for a moment but then he saw that the girl's hands were shaking badly.

'Put the gun down, Maggie,' he ordered her in a low, calm voice. 'I know you're scared, but I ain't gonna harm you none.'

The girl hesitated for a moment and then lowered the gun so that it was now pointing at the floor.

He advanced on her slowly, like a mountain cat.

'It's your eyes, Maggie,' he told her. 'It's your eyes that show that you're scared.'

He was right — or almost. As long as the girl could see her small brother or even part of his body, she was afraid that she might miss and injure or kill him. But Randall was closing on her now and Luke was no longer visible, which meant he was safe. Randall stretched his hand out.

'The gun, Maggie,' he coaxed. 'Give me the gun.'

Instead, she jerked the Colt up suddenly. The look she gave the gunslinger now held no fear, only loathing. Realizing his mistake, Randall had to choose between lunging for her weapon or drawing his own gun. In that split second she fired and sent a slug crashing into his rib-cage. Randall keeled over and ended up on all fours on the ground. Even then he found the strength to reach for his .45. Maggie stood over him, her hands still smarting from the recoil of the Colt, and finished him off with a second shot that shattered his spine.

The girl looked towards the door. Millard was leaning against it, his cheek swollen and sore. Maggie's face was drained of colour.

'I knew he was here, Jess,' she said. 'I didn't need to be told. I could *feel* him.'

Then she fainted.

★　★　★

It wasn't till the following afternoon that Millard felt well enough to load the gunslinger's body onto the buckboard and take him into Reposo for burial. Lamont's foreman Lew rode into the homesteader's yard just before Millard was intending to set out. When he saw the corpse stretched out on the waggon Lew remarked drily,

'You've had a busy couple of days, Jess. Not one of them varmints got away.'

Millard nodded. 'How's Jamie Lamont and the others?' he asked.

'I took his ma and pa into town this morning to see him,' the foreman replied. 'Jamie's gonna be OK, so is his friend Victor Day who caught a slug in the shoulder. Big Ned wasn't so lucky. He'll be buried in the morning and I guess he deserves a good turn-out for it.'

'If they hadn't lent a hand I'd be a dead man,' Millard said sombrely.

'I think Jamie and them other youngsters are enjoying all the attention they're getting. There's one thing that's worrying Jamie, though,' Lew said.

'What's that?'

'After the fright you gave him for calling you yeller, Jamie vowed he'd never use the word again, but that's just what he did call Mathew Stag before Stag went out and gunned the last of Hollis's gang down in the street. Jamie was still feverish this morning and he went on and on about regretting what he said. He kept asking me if I reckon he'll ever really grow up to be a man like his father.'

'And do you?' Millard asked, knowing how fond Lew was of the Lamonts.

'I dunno, Jess,' the ranch foreman answered with a broad grin. 'What do you reckon . . . ?'

THE END